KARTHIKA NAÏR

UNTIL THE LIONS

Echoes from the Mahabharata

archipelago books

First Archipelago Books Edition, 2019

First published as *Until the Lions: Echoes from the Mahabharata*
by Harper Collins India, 2015

Archipelago Books
232 Third St. #A111
Brooklyn, NY 11215
www.archipelagobooks.org

Library of Congress Cataloging-in-Publication Data available upon request.

Distributed by Penguin Random House
www.penguinrandomhouse.com

Cover art: "Rediscovery of the Ashoka pillar in Sarnath,"
Archaeological Survey India, 1905
Cover design by Zoe Guttenplan. Interior design by Gopa & Ted2, Inc.

This book was made possible by the New York State Council on the Arts with the
support of Governor Andrew M. Cuomo and the New York State Legislature.

Archipelago Books also gratefully acknowledges the generous support from Lannan Foundation,
the Carl Lesnor Family Foundation, the Nimick Forbesway Foundation,
and the New York City Department of Cultural Affairs.

For Ennammachi, Achan & Amma,
my first mythologists

There is that great proverb – that until the lions
have their own historians, the history of the hunt
will always glorify the hunter. That did not come
to me until much later. Once I realized that, I had
to be a writer. I had to be that historian.
It's not one man's job. It's not one person's job.
But it is something we have to do, so that the story
of the hunt will also reflect the agony,
the travail – the bravery, even, of the lions.

CHINUA ACHEBE, *The Paris Review*
('The Art of Fiction', N° 139)

CONTENTS

UNTIL THE LIONS

UNTIL THE LIONS: OF MYTHS AND MEN

When I was nine, my father overheard me bragging to friends, children of his colleagues in the army. Though he had not been injured in battle, he had fought in all three wars India had waged in the 1960s and 70s, and been recognised for his work – feats I had been flaunting to secure my glazed brick on our particular social pyramid. Our lot had rather grim measures of hierarchy: so, the classmate whose parent had lost a limb in a bomb blast easily held the capstone; the rest of us were scrabbling below.

After he walked into our vicarious contest, my father didn't say much. That night, though, he quietly shared a few thoughts, memories, with me. First, that there were no altruistic battles, that countries engaged in warfare out of self-interest. There was nothing celebratory about military combat, he said: it was – at best – a necessary evil, all too often initiated in a show of political or national pride; once in a while, to defend land and freedom. Whatever the reason, it was undertaken at almost immeasurable cost.

There were, he said, few noble victors in war, seldom real 'saviour armies'. Victory could stoke horrible reactions in human beings: it encouraged pillage and abuse even in ordinarily principled people. When men became conquerors, he said, they often paid for it by losing part of their humanity, only they didn't know it immediately. He didn't ever want to hear me boasting about his war record, because he had done what was necessary at that point, what many thousands of people had to. But it was not something one should want to relive, nor brandish as an achievement.

Most of what he explained did not make sense immediately; in fact, what I had felt then was a bewildered indignation that he would not let me crow about such exciting deeds. Yet, the words stayed close, sounding louder and clearer over time, as events around the world – in Ireland, Iraq, Bosnia, Rwanda, Sri Lanka, Kashmir, Manipur, closer and closer home – served to provide a brutal, ever-growing illustration.

By the time I began to write *Until the Lions*, those words had become an ostinato inside my head, with fragments echoing in various keys. Those words were ones I heard no more outside memory, as my father (like much of the world around him) gradually shifted to hawkish convictions about national identity and army impunity, and a growing distrust in the need for dissent.

Each of the characters in the book views one or more of the triggers and upshots of war through separate vantage points, whose existence I learnt from my father's earlier, farsighted self. Each brings a reminder of the moral and physical price exacted on and outside the battlefield – in victory and defeat – by the unnamed wellspring of warfare: militant patriarchy. A patriarchy which demands ownership, appropriation: of land, of wealth, of qualities like heroism and honour, and, inevitably, of bodies, especially those considered an inferior other. Indigenous communities, 'lower' castes, women.

Women. As another soldier remarked, throughout history women are among the first casualties of war and conflict. Their bodies become territories: possessed, ravaged, ploughed as though for produce, discarded, carelessly destroyed. But, unlike with land, the stigma of conquest is attached to their person; they become repositories of lost honour, individual and collective.

Salman Rushdie wrote most memorably on this in *Shame*, on the strange – and expedient – transfer of subjugation and dishonour from the men who've experienced defeat to the women who will suffer the consequences of that defeat and bear its scars on their bodies. Narratives across time echo this enduring practice of violence and violation inflicted on women, whether through Briseis and Cassandra in Homer's *Iliad*, Sita and Shoorpanaka in Valmiki's *Ramayana*, or the daughters of El Cid in *El Poema de mio Cid*.

But why the Mahabharata: that is a question asked frequently. After all, this age scarcely has a shortage of accounts of large-scale conflicts and their aftermath. Why not write a brand-new story, anchored by the present, set in an identifiable place?

Perhaps because foundational epics remain instantly identifiable. They contain the essence of the human experience, whichever the era or continent they are (re)discovered in, and however different the civilisation. They reflect the richness and complexity of humankind, its capacity for betrayal, cruelty, enduring hate, and also for breath-taking generosity and love. They know the cadences of the human heart and can deliver them through universally recognisable, even familiar, chords. Ambition, greed, arrogance, envy.

Tenderness, desire, loyalty, sacrifice. Foundational epics highlight them all, their conflicting presence, within the same characters – sometimes within the same chapter.

And the Mahabharata, specifically? Like many Asians, I would be hard-pressed to say just when this epic first flew across my consciousness, how it found a permanent perch there. Was it during intricate all-night kathakali performances where gods, heroes and villains – resplendent in ornate costumes and fiery masks – descended on stage to effortlessly own attention and memory? Through thunderous fantasy films? Nightly sessions in pre-school years with a raconteur great-aunt? Was it a recital of Ved Vyaasa's text, deemed the original, or a regional variation, Tamil, Bhil, Javanese…? Or Amar Chitra Katha comics – those early conduits to myth, legend and history for generations of Indians (region, religion, language no bar)?

As children, we each had our favourite: hypnotic Krishna, god incarnate; genial, gluttonous Bheema; brave, tormented Karna, caught between friend and family; beautiful, outspoken Draupadi…

Then, as we grow up, the Mahabharata begins to play tricks. It begins to resemble a kaleidoscope: shake the tube and patterns that emerge one minute will be nothing like what you saw an instant earlier. The bits and bobs inside will be the same – glass, feathers, leaves, thread – but positions shift, the view alters. Those beloved heroes? We find they have feet of flesh and blood, skin and nerves. But here is the rub: they become more intriguing, fascinating even; protagonists that cannot be pegged into slots, ones that challenge definitions of integrity and fairness, others that infuriate with noose-tight codes of caste hierarchy and expedient social order.

There is another reason for choosing the Mahabharata as the source for *Until the Lions*, even over its illustrious sibling-epic, the Ramayana. In the Mahabharata, the enemy – to be destroyed at all cost – is not some distant, savage Other whose alienation, whose moral divergence, can be ascribed to convenient divides like race, creed, ideology… No, that mortal enemy is one's own kin; the blood the heroes spill is all their own. And, seen from diverse angles, these antagonists are variously recognised as brave, generous and noble, even worthy claimants to the throne. Therein lies another rub. Right and wrong are not so easy to spot any more. Is duty, so central to the epic, a pretext for acts of unspeakable violence? Can hatred overtake all other emotions, reasons, to become the motor in a war allegedly for justice?

Persistent, irresistible questions. Especially when there are multiple sets of lenses to view them with, and a landscape with contours that could fit into almost any age or territory in human history, including the history we witness today.

Yet, the Mahabharata would have simply remained my favourite destination as a reader and viewer, with innumerable adaptations and variations to savour, from the sublime to the absurd, had it not been for two triggers in early 2010. The first – a novel that recast the equation between two protagonists, heroic and wilful – had exasperated with one-dimensional portraits of champions and villains, yet lingered, stoking a nebulous desire to celebrate the depth and ambiguity in those characters instead.

A month later, I read *Sarpa Satra*, the late Arun Kolatkar's electrifying book-length poem which revisits the epic through the eyes of serpents massacred in the sacrifice bookending Vyaasa's *Mahabharata*. Not only did Kolatkar train a savagely funny gaze on humanity's perceptions of its own heroism and superiority, he brilliantly, casually, underscored how timeless the ethical questions raised by the epic are. *Sarpa Satra* tells of the ease and righteousness with which the most civilised of societies can unleash carnage that will only later be defined genocide. Without resorting to obvious devices like time travel, it provides a dismal snapshot of the directions in which a combination of narcissistic leadership, servile administration and corporate greed could take today's democratic nation-state. All this in roughly a hundred prescient pages.

Strange things happened that day. Axons were galvanised, synapses broke apart, then rewired themselves. The pulse screamed. It was painful, visceral. Thrilling. So, it may have been in a state of biochemical inebriety that I met Karthika V.K., my first – and namesake – editor-publisher: my next book would be a re-imagining of the Mahabharata through the voices of eighteen women, I had told her, on that first day. Eighteen for the eighteen parva – the books – that constitute the epic. But also for the days of the war that forms its narrative crux. It would be in verse, I had added emphatically, and each voice would represent one parva. It would traverse time and place, I continued, and be located across various epochs and continents. (I am not sure how or why Karthika kept a straight face through this fearsomely convoluted proposal, but she did.)

Five years later, when she finally had my manuscript in hand, Karthika V.K. gently, valiantly, forbore to comment that she had an altogether other beast to deal with.

For one, the book began with the birth of Satyavati (thereby eliding 6 of the 19 sub-books of the *Adi Parva,* and several dozen generations of ancestors), Vyaasa's mother, who – with little heed for authorial blueprints and wishes – became the central narrative voice, the connective tissue that binds most of the chronicle together.

Then, the stories were not evenly distributed across chronology. The last few parva – recounting the Pandava reign after the great war, and their final journey to hell and heaven – featured nowhere.

There were nineteen voices, instead of the symbolic – and promised – eighteen, oh, with three belonging to male characters, one to a dog, and another to a serpent-queen.

(Time and space travel had vanished entirely, though that provided immediate, all-round relief.)

Until the Lions is nowhere near a comprehensive retelling of the Mahabharata that included all eighteen parva or even a complete, linear account of the lives of the Kurus. The word *echoes*, thus, was added as subtitle to describe this assemblage of fragments. For these are the remains of the voices that clamoured most to me, some magnified, some refracted, some residual.

The book was not the only thing to have transformed "between the idea and the reality." The world had, in startlingly swift, near-unrecognisable ways, between 2010 and 2015. Many widely chronicled, the horrific signposts that impale the first fraction of this century: Al-Qaeda, then Daesh; authoritarian rulers, backed by guns or the ballot; a tidal wave of majoritarianism. Other markers were quieter, perilously incremental – closer home, each time.

In 2011, painter M.F. Husain died of a heart attack, in exile, far from his native India: he had fled to Doha, and then London, following death threats, and multiple charges of obscenity and offending religious sentiment, all on account of his nude portraits of Hindu gods and goddesses. (Why this should cause outrage in the 21st century when Indian iconography, ancient and otherwise, has been no stranger to divine nudes is a glaring – and distressing – question.)

A few months later, *Three Hundred Ramayanas: Five Examples and Three Thoughts on Translation* – the late poet and translator A.K. Ramanujan's luminous, insightful essay exploring the journey taken by that epic across Asia over two millennia – was removed from the syllabus of Delhi University, this one too because of "protests from hardline Hindu groups and a number of teachers."*

Around the same time, in a reminder that intolerance and opportunism are great global levellers, here in Paris the Catholic fundamentalist party Renouveau National staged violent protests (which included the hurling of stink bombs, eggs and oil at theatre-goers) outside Théâtre de la Ville where Romeo Castellucci's performance "Sul concetto di volto nel figlio di Dio" was being staged. They claimed the sets – featuring the face of Christ that progressively became sullied – were covered in excrement, despite clarifications to the contrary from the director. The play, revolving around an ageing man and his caregiver son, poignantly, painstakingly, chronicles the frailty of the flesh and relationships, human or divine. Facts seldom interest agitators, optics do.

Of course, none of it was really new. And few regimes, few leaders – from emperors Augustus and Qin Shi Huang to the modern-day, democratic governments of Rajiv Gandhi, Sir John Keys or Barack Obama – unequivocally espouse the cause of freedom of expression, certainly not when it can make things difficult for them. Fewer nations react, as a people, to attacks against this particular fundamental right: there is a vague, uneasy idea that it is an elitist (sometimes called "first-world") privilege, an optional requirement. Belief – religious, racial, national – is generally considered more fragile, more noble – worthier of protection – than individual expression.

By 2015, attacks were not limited to charges, removal from a curriculum, or stink bombs at shows.

By 2015, casualties were not statistics anymore, reported with increasing urgency by PEN or FreeMuse. They were names, faces, voices you knew, had read, watched, heard. Some, those first met when young – in the flesh, or

*Soutik Biswas reporting for BBC World: https://www.bbc.com/news/world-south-asia-15363181

through words, chords, images – and dearly loved. Artists, writers, activists: some whose work, whose life had powered your own, from near or far. People who had merely gone out one day to celebrate art and debate, laughter and sport. Narendra Dabholkar. Ahmed Rajib Haider. Gulnar (Muskan). Bernard Maris. Govind Pansare. Avijit Roy. 21 visitors to Bardo National Museum. H Farook. M M Kalburgi. Francisco Hernández. 89 music-lovers attending an *Eagles of Death Metal* gig at Bataclan.

The living are targeted in other ways. With book bans. Prison. Exile. Fatwa. Smear campaigns. Accusations of sedition… Kamel Daoud. Oleg Sentsov. Perumal Murugan. Atena Farghadani. Fatima Naoot. The 50-odd Indian writers (followed by film-makers and artists) – who had returned awards and honours as protest against the spate of murders of intellectuals and minorities – hounded as anti-nationals by several media houses and right-wing politicians.

By 2015, it was happening in cities as far-flung as Pune and Peshawar and Paris, Tamazula and Tunis. Closer and closer home. Close enough to turn and touch.

What does all this have to do with *Until the Lions*? There's that old proverb, "it takes a village to raise a child." To state the obvious, books are like that: the entire world pours into them, in different ways. Not just through the author as s/he fashions it, but the reader too, whether lay person, academic, critic or jury. This book received more love and attention than any of us expected. And the questions came fast and, sometimes, furious.

How dare you suggest Krishna acted unjustly in the war? Could you write this book in India? Aren't you projecting feminist aspirations on these characters? And my favourite: *Does a modern political sensibility or subaltern/minority narrative have any validity when interpreting a sacralised worldview with a unique epistemology?*

There have been less polite, more, well, rhetorical ones too.

Here is the thing: this book is the mutant, happily illicit child of many ancestors, with varied provenance. Vyaasa himself, whose *Mahabharata* contains something as radical as an entire book – the Stree Parva – chronicling the laments and tirades of the grieving mothers and widows of both warring clans in the wake of the final carnage. Ovid, with his millennia-old *Heroides*, where the women from Greek and Roman mythology own their stories in passionate, eloquent epistles.

Amir Khusrau, who could sing to his spiritual master in Persian and Braj, alternating languages within the same couplet. Andal of the fierily sensual poetry for her beloved deity, Perumal.

Bhâsa, who – almost two thousand years ago – adapted plays from the epics, ones where the motives of the gods are openly challenged, ones imagining alternative scenarios, including a pacifist King Duryodhana who loves his enemy's son as dearly as his own. The 9th century Tamil poet Perunthevanar, whose telling of the Mahabharata, *Parata Venpa*, highlights the life and ultimate sacrifice of Aravan, Arjuna's snake-prince son.

Subaltern narratives? A political sensibility? They are as ancient and new, as *valid*, as the human imagination which can be ascribed neither to the 21st century nor the First World nor any religion or ideology. All these writers – and innumerable others – told and retold, questioned and changed the stories, the narratives they had inherited. They reshaped the old, they crafted the new, and whatever the environment – often encouraging, often unforgiving, for resistance to invention is just as ancient as the creative act – they continued, however they could. They knew that there were no small freedoms, and that the imagination would be the most priceless gift to give up. For how else can we attempt to understand what it is to be another, god or soldier, woman or wolf? What else can allow us to sense the many ways there are to inhabit the earth? To envision a better reality?

Until the Lions begins with a proverb Chinua Achebe quoted widely. There is one more that comes to mind now. *The world is like a mask dancing. If you want to see it well, you do not stand in one place.*

FAMILY TREE

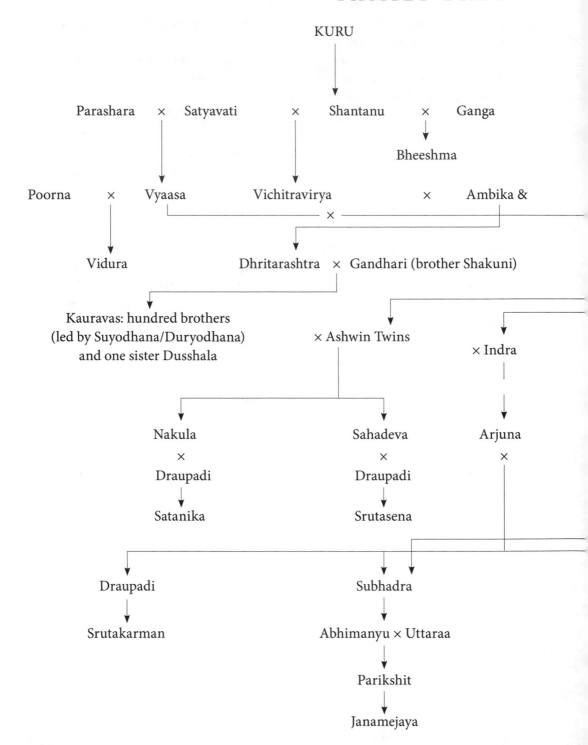

OF THE KURU DYNASTY

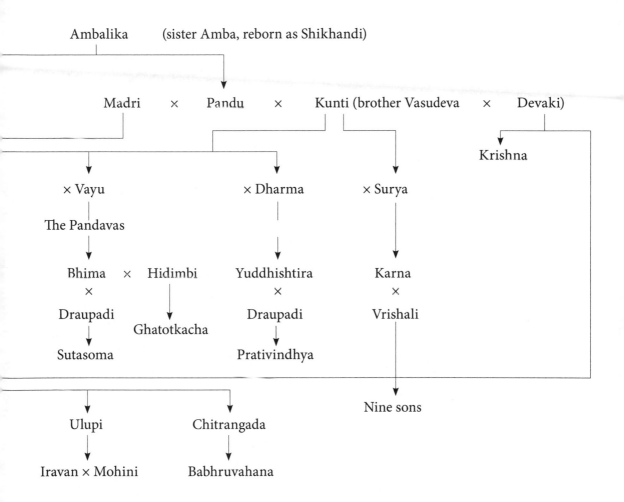

Ambalika   (sister Amba, reborn as Shikhandi)

Madri × Pandu × Kunti (brother Vasudeva × Devaki)

Krishna

× Vayu   × Dharma   × Surya

The Pandavas

Bhima × Hidimbi   Yuddhishtira   Karna
×   ×   ×
Draupadi   Draupadi   Vrishali
          Ghatotkacha
Sutasoma   Prativindhya

Nine sons

Ulupi   Chitrangada

Iravan × Mohini   Babhruvahana

DRAMATIS PERSONAE

ABHIMANYU: Heir to the throne of Hastinapur as the oldest 'royal' Pandava grandchild, Abhimanyu is the only child of Arjuna and Subhadra, Krishna's younger sister. On the 13th day of the Kurukshetra war, he is killed in unfair combat by the Kaurava forces, outnumbered and isolated within the padmavyuha, a deadly battle formation – a trap he enters at his uncles' behest.

AMBA/SHIKHANDI: The eldest princess of Kashi, Amba is abducted (along with her two sisters) on her wedding day by Bheeshma, regent of the Kuru Kingdom, and offered as bride to his brother, Vichitravirya. The abduction ruins Amba's life: her betrothed rejects her when she returns to him, and Bheeshma, too, refuses to marry her. Unable to get justice from any mortal, Amba invokes the gods. After many years of austerities, Shiva appears and grants her the power to kill Bheeshma, but only in her next life. Amba kills herself to hasten her retribution and is later reborn as the princess of Panchala, Shikhandi, who finally acquires manhood from a kind-hearted demigod, a yaksha.

AMBIKA: Amba's younger sister, Ambika weds Vichitravirya – the Kuru crown prince – after her abduction. Impregnated by Ved Vyaasa after her husband's death, she gives birth to Dhritarashtra.

AMBALIKA: The youngest of the Kashi princesses, Ambalika weds Vichitravirya as well. She, too, is made to have a child from Ved Vyaasa, a son named Pandu.

ARAVAN: Also known as Iravan (in Vyaasa's Mahabharata), Aravan is the son of the Naga queen Ulupi and Arjuna, conceived during Arjuna's first exile from Hastinapura. In many Tamil versions of the Mahabharata (particularly those of the Koothandavar cult), Aravan, who joins the Pandava army during the Kurukshetra war, is asked to offer himself as a ritual sacrifice to the goddess Kali – one that will ensure Pandava victory.

Arjuna/Partha: The third Pandava brother, Kunti's son from Indra, king of gods. Arjuna spends his entire life perfecting his skills as an archer and bedding beautiful, powerful women in different parts of the planet, often begetting sons he seems to forget all about until the war.

Bhanumati: The wife of Duryodhana (the Kaurava crown prince); and princess of Kalinga.

Bheeshma: Born to the Kuru king Shantanu and the river-goddess Ganga, Bheeshma – known as Devavrata in his youth – is one of the eight Vasus or elemental gods, cursed by the sage Vashishta to spend a lifetime on earth following the kidnapping of Kamadhenu, a very holy cow. He gets the name Bheeshma – or He of the Terrible Oath – following his vow of celibacy.

Bheema: The second Pandava prince, born to Kunti and Vayu, lord of the winds. Bheema is renowned for both his appetite and his strength. He vows to kill his hundred Kaurava cousins after the game of dice and the disrobing of Draupadi – an oath he upholds during the Kurukshetra war.

Chitrangada: There are at least three Chitrangadas in the Mahabharata. The first is Shantanu and Satyavati's son, Bheeshma's half-brother, the Kuru prince who is killed by another Chitrangada – a gandharva or demigod, who cannot bear the thought of a mortal namesake. The third Chitrangada is a beautiful warrior-queen from northeast India who marries Arjuna during one of his many exiles.

Dhrishtadhyumna: Prince of Panchala, and son of King Dhrupad. Dhrupad propitiates the gods to acquire a son who will avenge his defeat at the hands of Drona, childhood friend turned foe. Dhrishtadhyumna, along with his twin sister Draupadi, is born from that yagna or sacrificial fire.

Dhritarashtra: Kuru king, the son that Queen Ambika begets from Ved Vyaasa. Dhritarashtra is born blind. He is denied the throne initially due to his disability, a decision that embitters him and generates much of the later enmity between his sons and nephews.

DHRUPAD: King of Panchala, father of Shikhandi, Dhrishtadhyumna and Draupadi. His enmity with Drona becomes the driving force of his life after the latter sends his pupils to defeat Dhrupad and annex half of his kingdom. He engineers Draupadi's marriage to Arjuna, in the hope that he can avenge his humiliation one day with the help of the Pandavas.

DRONACHARYA: or Drona, the preceptor of the Pandavas and Kauravas, is an invincible warrior, a master of warfare and divine weapons called astras. A childhood playmate of Dhrupad, Drona begins to hate the king after the latter refuses to recognise their friendship, on Drona's arrival at the Panchala court, impoverished and desperate. Dhrupad's defeat in war and the annexation of half his kingdom is the guru dakshina or teacher's fee that Drona demands of his royal pupils.

DRAUPADI (PANCHALI): Princess of Panchala, daughter of Dhrupad, and sister of Dhrishtadhyumna and Shikhandi, Draupadi later weds the five Pandava brothers and becomes the queen of Indraprastha. She suffers great humiliation – an attempted public disrobing – at the hands of the Kauravas when Yuddhishtira stakes her in a game of dice where he loses all his "possessions", including himself and his brothers.

DURYODHANA (*see* **SUYODHANA**)

DUSSHALA: The only daughter of Gandhari and Dhritarashtra, youngest sister to the hundred and one Kauravas. Dusshala marries Jayadratha, the king of Sindhu, who joins the Kaurava side during the Kurukshetra War.

DUSHASANA: The second of the hundred sons of Dhritarashtra and Gandhari. Vyaasa represents Dushasana as a thoroughly villainous character, with – unusually – no redeeming feature. His attempted disrobing of Draupadi in the Hastinapur court is one of the triggers to the Kurukshetra war, spurring Bheema's vow to kill all hundred Kaurava brothers, and specifically, to disembowel Dushasana and wash Draupadi's tresses in his blood.

EKALAVYA: A Nishada (tribal) prince who seeks to become the best archer in the world. Spurned by the royal guru, Drona, as an outcast, Ekalavya builds a bust of the man, considers the clay image his teacher and goes on to excel in archery, surpassing even Arjuna, who reigns unbeaten in the kshatriya world. As payment for his symbolic training, Drona demands that Ekalavya cut off the thumb of his right hand, which would effectively prevent him from wielding the bow anymore.

GANDHARI: The Princess of Gandhar who is made to marry the blind king Dhritarashtra. Gandhari is celebrated for her devotion: according to Vyaasa's Mahabharata, she blindfolds herself when she learns that her future husband is sightless. She only removes the blindfold once before her death.

GANGA: The river-goddess, created from waters of the Cosmic Ocean when Vishnu dug a hole in the universe with his toenail. Ganga too has to spend a short while on earth, birthing the Vasus (of whom Bheeshma is one), as punishment for sharing lustful glances with a mortal – Shantanu in an earlier life – while in Indra's court.

GHATOTKACHA: A rakshasa prince, son of Hidimbi and Bheema, Ghatotkacha is actually the oldest Pandava grandson, although he is never considered heir to the throne because of his mixed blood. He comes to the Pandavas' aid during their thirteen-year exile, and also at Kurukshetra, where his army and he wreak havoc on the Kauravas until he is killed by Karna's divine astra, Shakti, on the fourteenth night of war.

HIDIMBI: A rakshasi or demoness who later rules the forest Hidimbavana, Hidimbi is the sister of Hidimba, its cruel, man-eating king. She becomes Bheema's first wife: the Pandavas encounter her while fleeing from Varanavrata where their cousins tried to burn them alive in a lac palace. Hidimbi never tries to meet Bheema once the Pandavas leave Hidimbavana, but she sends her son Ghatotkacha and his men to support the Pandavas during the Kurukshetra war. She is still worshipped as a goddess in parts of Himachal Pradesh.

INDRA: The king of gods, god of thunder and lightning; a possessive, mercurial ruler who spends much of his long reign cursing nymphs and mortals.

KARNA: Kunti's oldest son, born to her and Surya, the sun god. Kunti, then unmarried and very young, casts away the infant. Karna is found and adopted by a charioteer, Adhiratha, and his wife Radha. His life is defined by the caste of his adopted parents, and he meets resistance and humiliation at every turn, especially when he seeks to train as a warrior. Duryodhana, recognising his unusual talent and worth, befriends him and crowns him as the (vassal) king of Anga. Karna swears eternal allegiance in return and stands by Duryodhana, even after secretly learning his parentage on the eve of the war.

KAURAVA: Technically, all the descendents of Kuru are Kauravas. But the term is used specifically to refer to the hundred (and one – except Yuyutsu was seldom included in the count) sons of Dhritarashtra.

KIRMIRA: The rakshasa king of Kamyaka forest, Kirmira is a dear friend of Hidimbi and the brother of Baka, another demon to be killed by Bheema. He comes across the Pandavas during their thirteen-year exile following the game of dice, and is killed by Bheema.

KRISHNA/ MOHINI: Krishna, the eighth incarnation of Vishnu, is a Yadava chieftain and cousin of the Pandavas, considered one of the most powerful gods in the modern Hindu pantheon. Kingmaker nonpareil, he guides most of the actions of the Pandavas, especially during the course of the war. When no woman agrees to marry Aravan before his sacrifice, Krishna transforms into a woman, Mohini the Enchantress, to marry the Naga prince and to mourn his death.

KUNTI: One of the queens of Hastinapura, widow of Pandu and mother of Karna and the five Pandavas, Kunti hails from the Yadava tribe and is also Krishna's paternal aunt.

LAKSHMANA: Duryodhana's firstborn, heir to the Kaurava throne. Killed by Abhimanyu, his cousin, on the twelfth day of war.

MADRI: Pandu's second wife, Madri is the princess of Madra. She dies on Pandu's funeral pyre, overcome with guilt at having accidentally catalysed his death – coitus being fatal for Pandu.

NAKULA: The fourth Pandava brother, and Madri's son from the Ashwin twins, divine physicians.

PADATI: A name given to foot soldiers, the greatest casualty of the Mahabharata. Padatis are urged to join the war on the pretext that martyrdom on Kurukshetra ensures direct access to heaven, and freedom from the cycle of death and rebirth and caste.

PANDU: King of the Kurus for a short while, Pandu is Queen Ambalika's son from Ved Vyaasa. He is also officially – though not biologically – the father of the five Pandava brothers.

PANDAVA: the term given to Pandu's five sons.

PARASHARA: A great seer, author of some of the founding Hindu scriptures, including the Puranas, and, according to Satyavati, an attentive and bountiful lover, who gives her a son, Ved Vyaasa – and some other practical boons.

POORNA: The dasi or handmaiden who takes Ambika's place the second time the latter is ordered by Satyavati to sleep with Ved Vyaasa. Poorna gives birth to Vidura, the only healthy child among the sons sired by Vyaasa. In Vyaasa's Mahabharata, Poorna remains nameless – perhaps because she never divulges her identity to him.

SAHADEVA: The fifth Pandava brother, and Madri's second (also twin) son from the Ashwin twins, divine physicians.

SATYAVATI: The fisher-princess whose beauty and determination change the course of the Kuru destiny; wife of King Shantanu, and mother of Ved Vyaasa, Chitrangada and Vichitravirya.

SAUVALI: The dasi whom Dhritarashtra chooses as concubine during Gandhari's pregnancy. Sauvali has a son from this forced liaison, Yuyutsu, who later becomes a key ally of the Pandava brothers.

SHAKUNI: Prince of Gandhara, brother of Gandhari, and catalyst of the enmity between the Pandavas and Kauravas. Every heinous deed by Duryodhana, every assassination attempt, every bit of chicanery or duplicity is shown as directly influenced or orchestrated by Shakuni. Yet, he, too, has a reason for unleashing so much hatred among the Kuru cousins.

SHANTANU: Kuru king, descendant of the lunar dynasty and forefather of the Pandavas and Kauravas – in a manner of speaking. His inability to resist dazzling – and purposeful – women, first Ganga and later Satyavati, would appear to be his defining trait.

SHUNAKA: An independent-minded canine, one of the earliest of the species. Shunaka is wary of the human race, but not more than of gods and seers, and is averse to the idea of unconditional allegiance to any race. She remembers the past and the future and warns her kin against a close association with mankind. *NB*: Shunaka is the only fully invented character in this collection: while the myths and ancestors she mentions, the incidents that she invokes, are all recorded in Vyaasa's Mahabharata or in the Vedas and Puranas, Shunaka herself is a figment of this author's imagination.

SUYODHANA (also known as **DURYODHANA**): The eldest of the hundred Kaurava princes, son of Dhritarashtra and Gandhari. Suyodhana's hatred and distrust of his cousins, the Pandavas, is the main source of conflict in Hastinapura, prompting the partition of the kingdom, and later, the Kurukshetra war between the two sides of the family.

ULUPI: Queen of the Nagas, and mother of Aravan. It is Ulupi who grants Arjuna the boon of invincibility in water.

UTTARAA: Princess of Matsya, the kingdom where the Pandavas seek refuge, incognito, during their thirteenth year of exile. She is married off to

Abhimanyu, the Pandava crown prince, as part of the pre-war alliance strategy of the Pandavas to garner support from powerful kingdoms.

VED VYAASA (Krishna Dvaipavana Vyaasa): The son of Parashara and Satyavati, Ved Vyaasa is considered the author of the original Mahabharata, and the man who divided the Vedas into four and compiled and edited them. He fathered Dhritarashtra, Pandu and Vidura in his spare time.

VICHITRAVIRYA: The second son of Satyavati and Shantanu, and husband of Ambika and Ambalika. He dies quite early in the story, and his greatest contribution to the narrative is to ratchet up the tension by dying childless.

VIDURA: Ved Vyaasa's son from Ambika's maid, who later becomes Prime Minister of the Kuru kingdom. Vidura is considered the epitome of wisdom and statecraft.

VRISHALI: Karna's wife, who belongs to the suta – charioteer and storyteller – community, like Karna's adopted parents. Vrishali loses her husband and eight of her nine sons in the Mahabharata war. She commits sati on Karna's pyre.

YUDDHISHTIRA: Kunti's oldest legitimate son, born of her coupling with Yama, the god of death and dharma. Considered the embodiment of all kingly virtue, Yuddhishtira enjoys the unstinting support and loyalty of his mother and Pandava brothers, despite some appalling actions like staking his brothers and their common wife in a dice game (and losing them).

YUYUTSU: Yuyutsu is Dhritarashtra's son from the maid Sauvali. Raised alongside the Kauravas, Yuyutsu is nonetheless always treated as a half-caste and illegitimate son. From childhood, he turns informant for his cousins, the Pandavas, and apprises them of the Kaurava plots against them, including assassination attempts. On the first day of the Kurukshetra War, he crosses sides to fight with the Pandavas. He is the only son of Dhritarashtra to survive the war, the one to perform the last rites for all his fallen kin.

SATYAVATI

I. FAULT LINES

Listen. Listen: hate rises, hate blazes, hate billows
from battlefields. Hate arrives – searing rivers,
shrivelling plains, reaping deserts on its path –
even to this doorstep, to rule the roost, now hate
arrives to gorge our mountains in serpentine
maws, to smother fir and spruce and hemlock, to
parch my blameless sky into white dust so embers
fall as stars. Hate dissevers takin and goral,
black bear, weaver, deer, leopard and dragonfly
harboured by this hermitage, hate blanches your
still-human eyes, flows down larynx and pharynx
and trachea, leadens the breath and whirlpools
memory's voice till all you know all you feel all
you seek is nothingness. Old hate, descended
from heavens, leavened on my land. Old hate,
diffused through blood and womb and semen.
Old hate that I too begat, old hate bequeathed
and bartered, won in battle, given as bride-price,
hate that blighted six generations of this clan,
deforming husbands, grandsons, aunts and
nephews, brides and celibates, hate that only one
soul eludes, a baseborn sainted bard – Vyaasa,
my lone living son Vyaasa – with words to hymn
this story across millennia while birth and death
and love and youth jostle for place, while hate, old
hate, spores and multiplies.

In Kurukshetra
the Earth swathes her face in blood,
Death begins to dance.

PADATI

I. The Father

PAWN TALK: BRASS AND STRING

This is Kurukshetra, Son.
This is where our kings seek
to die – kings, princes, generals,
that whole heedless race of high-
born war-mongers – for a skyway,
swift and direct to heaven. Theirs, you
say, their heaven, not ours, it will still
be their heaven, as it is their earth,
their honour, both already theirs,
and with lives so slaked, heaven
their only conquest left.

But this is Kurukshetra,
this is where things could
change, Son. I heard the sages
swear: equal will all men be, in hell
or heaven, once killed here. Think, if
even the pariahs – Mahar and Shanar,
Chamar and Chandal, Dhobi, Bhangi,
they whose shades taint the land, so
the scholars also swear – can attain
casteless paradise, such an honour
once slain, perhaps our lives too
shall stand another chance
on so holy a strand

as Kurukshetra, sculpted
by Shiva's own hand, then laid
east of Maru, rainless Maru, north
of wild Khandava, where Takshaka
rules his crafty tribe, south of gentle
Turghna yet westerly, not too far from
Parin. Dharmakshetra, they call her too,
this curl between two sacred rivers –
Saraswati and Dhrishtadvati – that
traverse the eight known worlds,
gleaning virtues – alongside all
the silt and loam and rubble –
from each one to disperse
on the divine hearse

that is Kurukshetra.
On these sands, they'd
abound: satya, daya, daan,
kshama, tapas, suchi …Truth,
Largesse, Purity, then – to uncurse
generations still to be sown – Mercy
and Kindness, Son, oh, and Celibacy,
Sacrifice, and some other merits I
can never name throng to make
this Vishnu's ground, its godly
name his gift to an early,
devout Kuru king.

Look, on Kurukshetra,
night rises like another sun,
a younger, more brilliant one.
To the west stands the Pandava
camp: Yuddhishtira's legions face
the break of each new dawn, theirs
the demand for war to attain peace
and justice, to retrieve his old realm,
the land he strewed with ease like
sand or dice, the subjects he cast
away in less than a trice. Crown
and honour should be his, our
elders persist, noble soul who
never lies, king with a single
vice: avid, unskilled player.

While Kurukshetra
can scarce contain the dark
constellation of Duryodhana's
army: his men – a dazzle of fearless
glory – suffuse the East, from centre
to brim. Good, kind Duryodhana, our
Kuru sovereign, ours, Son, like few have
ever been. Duryodhana, eldest of the one
and hundred mighty Kaurava sons of that
purblind king Dhritarashtra. Duryodhana,
far-sighted like few rulers ever care to be,
reaping not one, nor a few but thirteen
harvests of peace, safety, prosperity
for all his people, even those of us
that survive like vermin
on outer rims.

Of this Kurukshetra
do the sutas spin lore, Son:
of an earth engorged with astras,
rathas, rathis, maharathis, where tens
of millions ride to the fore (thousands
have to turn into several crores in ballads,
else how will heroes take wing and soar?)
flanked by jewel-studded beasts galore –
horses, tuskers, camels, nagas, even
rakshasas – while hounds, pack-
mules, raptors, drummers, flies,
devas and apsaras goggle
in sad delight, for on

Kurukshetra will unfold
the future of the human cause.
So declares Bheeshma, our Kuru
ancient, commander of the Kaurava
force (and who else would know?) to his
enemy other, the Panchal Yuvraaj, Prince
Drishtadhyumna, as they lay down the laws,
together, of righteous combat: who may
fight, with whom and against, how and
when and where or not. (Not why, alas:
do not ask why, that is a tenet no one
tallies.) But this war must, they aver,
stay a sacred compact, a dharma
yuddha. Thus, and thus alone,
the Elder adds, with no little
pride, as karma bhoomi

will Kurukshetra be
renowned in the chronicles
of humankind. So unrolls their
list, slow and scrupulous. Compeers
alone can fight: rathis must duel rathis,
Son, and spare charioteers; maharathis
maharathis, not lesser beings; sidekicks
may kill each other but not kings; foot-
soldiers shall not be speared by archers,
neither smashed by mace-fighters nor
mangled by tuskers in the name of
their royal masters. Honour, at all
times, must be all. This shall be
a glorious war, one the gods
will envy and emulate.

Why, on Kurukshetra's
concourse, warriors may
hack off heads, like anywhere
else, of course, but only of equals!
And those unfit, afraid, unarmed or
injured must always remain unharmed:
no dagger ever should aim a fleeing back,
no arrow should strike a neck unawares.
Oh, musicians, mounts (equine as well
as elephant), flag-bearers, women,
children and messengers must
never feel alarmed.

In Kurukshetra, Son,
words will joust with other
words while swords with swords
alone do battle. And they shall all
abstain when twilight swallows sun
and sky, to recommence only when
day alights once again. Honour shall
be the reigning queen, the One we
honour before god and kin. Good
will blight evil, the Elders predict,
and new gods will appear. Dark-
skinned beings, perhaps, like
you and me, perhaps – just
think – a lowborn one?

Kurukshetra changes
nothing, you rage. But pause,
pause for a second, Son, to consider
my words, untaught, innocent, tedious
as they seem. There is vast little I know,
beyond the lore you so loathe, but this I do
for sure: to stay alive, a man must believe
in something, Son, even if that thing be
death. Rage can only keep you alive
for so long. To breathe, I grab onto
this grail of a noble war that could
confer honour – and flight, can it
be? – to my blood. Yes, this is
my choice, we all need one
to call our own.

SPOUSES, LOVERS

CONSTANCY I

Before a battle,
grow inwards, like root and rock:
shed eyes, ears; shed words.
Let us speak, your skin to mine.
Touch alone ooores memory.

Touch alone will survive
Time

SATYAVATI

II. FAULT LINES

Listen. Listen, this neither begins nor ends
with me, not such a hate cascading down Time,
crossing sea and sky and continent, a hate that
sails beside friendship, love, fealty, so many skiffs.
I could not say where it began, perhaps only the
stars can, for beginnings come clothed in mist.
There are many who will claim to know, Vyaasa
foremost, but even saintly bards – especially when
sons – don't allow tales to travel unadorned.
And so I must uncage the quieter lore, let them
wander, rags and slander notwithstanding. There
may be rhyme but not much reason, little metre,
but both stress and distress. This is not the whole
story, nor a lyrical history of mankind:[1] it is what
I know to be mine, true, or nearly so, perhaps not
at all at times, for Truth is a beast more wayward
than Time.

So listen. Listen: once, I learnt, there was a king,
complete with queen, court and kingdom – these,
not to be heard but seen. One morning, let's say,
a rare, soft morning in beryl, claret and cream,
with the gods at play in some other clime, the king
went off to hunt, as kings are wont. He chased and
stalked, trapped, shot and killed. Having killed
and killed again, littered the land with dead hart
and doe, tiger, partridge, even crow, he thought of
his wife, his favoured sport and pastime, and felt a
sudden surge of sperm. Loath to lose a rich future
life, into a banyan leaf he came, a leaf he sealed, and
bade his falcon carry home to his queen. Perhaps

he then killed some more, perhaps he lay down to dream of greater glory but now we must follow the sperm's story. The bird, ambushed by a viler raptor when halfway home, was forced to drop the seed over a snaking, silver watercourse. Into the mouth of a thirsting fish it fell, and the next thing we know, nine months on, a fisherman – grizzled, but not slow – hauled her onto his bamboo-bottomed coracle: the pregnant, heaving, sperm-eating porpoise. Strange the spectacle he found, slicing her belly into two: twins, squalling, red-cheeked newborns, and minutes later, a buxom, breathing apsara in place of dead fish. Thrice and hard the naiad kissed him – leaving him a little lovelorn – then winged her way out of that cruel curse, singing out to the fisherman to take the bundle to the king. King and court, however, did not see two bairns – both winsome as honey, noisome as hell – but the crown prince and his stinky, squalling womb-warmer, now disposable. *Well, boys,* said the king, *can rule even if they smell like tombs but I have no use for a girl, unless she can be my consort – no, with daughters, it's safest to abort.* As reward for bringing back their prince, the fisherman won a cloudburst of gold, plus the girl-child, non-returnable. With two parting caveats, stark and cold: *call her Matsyagandhi, the fish-scented one; take her away, far away, from this land and our son.*

A princess, and half-divine, bred in a fisher shack, severed from a brother who'd never know her name – that destiny was mine, that and the relentless stench of shame. Hate came easy. Hate came young. Hate for the royal father whose uncaring choice sealed this fate, for a mother who didn't raise her voice, hate for the loyal foster parent who would praise the king at every meal, sparing me no detail of his lord's largesse, never caring once for – or even noting – a daughter's distress. Hate had the smell of dead mackerel; hate bore shades of teal. I wore it as unhealing wound. I wore it as seal. I bade my time.

Feral-eyed, two cranes
collide, claws blurring frontlines.
Wings vanish the sky.

III. FAULT LINES

Listen. Listen, they will say it was the Golden Age,
they will say it was a time when gods and men
were equal, or almost, they will say humans knew
no want, no strife, no rage, no hate, no cleavage
of birth or caste or sex in the eyes of god or state.
They lie. They lie. They lie or they are wilfully
blind. How quickly, how cocksurely Vyaasa and
his kind claim the rest were not far behind! The
twice-born with their chronicles sire the illusions
they profess to so decry – false their yarn, fickle
the lore. There was no Golden Age, or if there was,
the age reserved its ore for kings and brahmins,
served base metal to us lesser beings – hunters,
fishers, scavengers, untouchables. A gilded sight
it seems, even yellow crap, when perched on
lucent heights. When they descend and the reek's
unmistakable, priests and hermits begin to sing a
different tune.

Listen, I should know. I was sixteen and beautiful:
even the Yamuna, bustling hellcat of a river, told
me so. If it weren't for that awful stench of fish, I'd
have been heaven-sent, rapturous; but as one both
lowborn and malodorous, I was termed repellent.
Then one wintry day, a soundless morning, as
the sun ran amok filling the heavens with colour,
stroke by uneven stroke, a rishi appeared at our
shanty door, demanding my father row him
across to the further shore. Father, village chief
in his old age, wished to eat his rice and fish in
peace, and pushed me to do the deed in his place.

We looked at each other, the roving sage and I, and then I knew, I knew how to climb to my pinnacle. He stepped into my coracle, holding on to my hand, each pulse a rising drumroll under pallid mien. No sooner had I cast off than he make his bid. *I want you. I want you, I want every bit of you, your skin the glow of star-kissed night, the rippling rivulets of your tress, breasts that are twin demilunes, the velvet address between those legs…* I stopped the flow of his delight: *But Sage, this would be a sin. Thou art a son of Brahma, learned, godly; I am bred as Nishada. Our coupling would be unholy. Besides, people see us from the shore, they will laugh at thee for bedding beneath thy station. I cannot let this be a coition we will deplore.*

In an instant, we were hidden in mystic fog, covering even the boat and oar: fully invisible. He leant over, aroused, for a kiss. Resistants tend to get cursed, so I unbent – a bit. *But Sage, coitus should be memorable for both, and how will you find me delectable with this stink of dead fish? And think, Ô Sage, how can I be free to pleasure thee when fearful for my repute, of the smear and uproar there will be if I'm found to have lost my virginity?* Now fully engorged and ardent, the ascetic swore: *Three boons you win: the name Satyavati, Ô truthful one, and much renown. My son whom you'll bear instantly, while a virgin you stay till you wear a royal crown. Lambent, youthful,*

*fragrant you shall remain till your dying day. Now
relent before I turn insane.* It worked, better than
I'd planned. Jasmine, rose and saffron: they rose
from my skin like zephyr and spread – spread
eight miles all around, with a whiff of red earth
at dusk.

Arms and legs braided into one, mouth padlocked
with tongue, digits entwined, he heaved, I writhed,
we conjoined: it smelt of blood, it smelt of musk. It
was a strange time, the first, but no worse than I'd
imagined, the old sage had life in him and magic
tricks to smoothen his knife. Painlessly – oh, the
only time – and quick as a chime did the child
arrive, full-grown and – sadly – pedantic. He
named himself Ved Vyaasa, river of the sacred
scripts, bowed, then vanished in his ascetic
father's steps, leaving me with the aftertaste of
victory, the sweet odour of eternity. With just a
faint pang of regret, umbrage in sharper twinge
that both mage and son could walk so quickly
away, forget me completely, but it wasn't enough
to single and survey. No, there was too much to
savour, this time, to expend my stockpile of hate,
which, it appeared, did not take root in Vyaasa's
heart – perhaps, though, hate's just a deadly,
distant fruit to one who never met fear or loss or
disrepute.

Krishna's chariot
scythes a thousand soldier skulls.
In war, rules fray first.

: 44 :

IV. FAULT LINES

Listen. Listen, you'd think life would transmute overnight. I had become aromatic, luminescent; some would even moot irresistible. But my father by now was half-blind, and our people's fears were potent – alarmed by my reputed occult power, they fled to screaming distance. Rumour embraced me like vine; its tendrils overtook my voice, my fragrance. Priests and men landed at the riverbank, to be ferried, they claimed, but it was my story that was sought. They drew a blank, of course – this secret could not be bought, and the caste, the caste of fisher-folk, made most retreat. Some less timorous, a few rather sweet, did ask for my hand – four merchants, a yaksha, a monk. But the river-goddess sang to me in many tongues, both to praise and advocate. *Take them. Take them in joy. Relish your will, relish youth and grace in bed. Be bold and celebrate. To rule a man, and his land, you need to learn just how much to give and withhold.* Then said, *but save your hand for the better mate; a worthier, nobler offer is yet to be sprung.* A crown would be worth every wait, to replace the crown I'd lost when very young. I bade my time.

Listen, a couple of years went by – sailboats adrift on horse latitudes. Then it happened at twilight one spring: it was a king all right, a king out on solitary hunt. He stared shamelessly but had the grace to be blunt: *Lady, I don't know your name or race or family, but your face and frame are splendrous, and your fragrance, your fragrance has me possessed. I am King Shantanu of Hastinapur, scion of the Kuru clan. Put your hand in mine, and you will be my queen, not concubine.* I liked him for that. Had I been less steeped in loss, in distrust, the answer would have been pat. But my tongue was eager to thrust. *But what of our sons and grandsons, King? Will they sit on your throne? Can they rule and own the kingdom after you?* Quieter than a winter sun he grew, his gaze leached with pain, but he neither blustered nor beseeched, just rode off into the brewing night. The river remained silent, and I had no one else to tell me what all this meant. Three weeks later, at that very hour, the same chariot dashed to a stop before our home, bearing terror-struck charioteer and a dour, strapping teen – unfinished mirror to my vanished suitor – who lost no breath to vent his spleen: *I am Devavrata, son of Goddess Ganga and King Shantanu, crown prince of Hastinapur. And you are the siren who's drowned my father in torment. His nights and days are at standstill since he met you. His hours fill, he says, with visions of your toes, your lips, your scent and parts I choose to eclipse. He neither eats nor drinks; he cares little for foes and defeats. But think hard, lowborn strumpet, of the pitfalls of your ruse: he could have seized or abused you, he didn't. Play coy any more, woman, and I'll show you why not to toy with Kuru men!* Hate rose from sleep. Hate blazed in belly and lung. Hate billowed through blood and bile. Hate dripped onto my tongue. *Rude, foolish cub, your father is a man – unlike his son. He knows that to own a body gives no access to the heart. I'm no slice of land for your kin to possess, no tart to be cussed. Your father, yes, did offer to make me queen, but what can that mean, when it will end, as it must? What of my children? What lies ahead for them when you rise to the throne?* I know *your kind – here I rust, in this filthy hut, because a man like you couldn't see the fruit for the rind.*

Our words snarled. Our words glared. Our words circled, baying for full victory – bare-clawed, fanged, tentacled. Organs ripped. Blood trickled. A century passed in an instant, a war was fought and won or lost in silence. Then he disowned his birthright, dropped the offence, *I renounce my claim to the Kuru throne. Your sons can succeed. Just wed the king.* I could have left it at that. I should have left it at that. My fears were freed. Hate could recede. But I didn't. I didn't and an epoch underwent a seismic shift. *You may renounce crown and kingdom, but what of your sons, Prince? And what of their sons? How can you ensure there'll be no blood-soaked rift?* Perhaps I'd wanted to draw more than blood. Perhaps I'd wanted to gnaw his proud, young heart till he was no more than husk. His voice was clear, his voice was dusk – it girdled river, mountain, cloud and sky: *Your sons will have nothing to fear from the understains of my breath. I swear, before gods in heaven and men on earth, I swear to stay celibate until death.*

Time stops in his path
to watch Bheeshma in battle –
each arrow, a song.

V. FAULT LINES

Bheeshma. Bheeshma: He of the terrible, tungsten oath. That's how they renamed him, Devavrata, for plighting his troth to chastity, spurning manhood and monarchy in fealty to father and future brethren. The gods applauded, they loved children blighting lives with senseless vows for selfish kin. Bheeshma, they chanted – with gandharvas, rishis, apsaras in harmony. Bheeshma, lauded land and sea and sky; forests, oceans, glaciers. Bheeshma, the name seared in deep crannies of hell, pealed dark but clear as a temple bell from the throats of distant stars. Bheeshma, gifted near-invincibility, with renown till eternity by the gods for valour and filial sacrifice. Bheeshma, whose father the king, dearly pleased at his oath of abstinence – my bride-price – bequeathed a new boon, destined to curdle: the freedom to choose how and when to die.

Listen. Listen, you'd think I'd won the sweeps: from fisher-maid to queen in the blink of an eye, and guaranteed queen-motherhood soon after. But he ensured victory didn't come cheap, Bheeshma. A lie I couldn't immure – the falsehood our first compact together. That was the fee, and it was steep: a lie that cast my father – gentle, clueless fisher-king – as raptor in every age. For when gods and numens had blessed and left the page, when land and sea and day had ended their warble, Bheeshma resumed, emotionless: *We have one thing left to settle. And it's a step you'll want to*

reject, but I insist, for Kuru pride I must protect –
despite your own lack of worth. The subjects will
resent a lowborn royal bride, but if they know what
you asked, they'll be merciless. No one must think
my celibacy was your demand: our queens are to be
unstained, virtuous. It is your father we must brand
as rapacious. I demurred, yes, but not enough. I
could have called his bluff, flaunted my obstinacy,
taken on court and kingdom undaunted. But I
didn't, I played along. I played along. I let down
my foster clan. And, in every version of the tale
that was spawned, the old fisherman laid down
this odious stipulation. From Vyaasa to his scribe,
the elephant-god, to his later tribe of bards – they
all had a handy pawn to fit the mould. For the
rest, it was as Bheeshma had foretold. The people
loathed me at first rumour. Worshippers of their
river-goddess queen, they clamoured I was no
more than a drain. It took a while, but once my
heavenly scent had done the job, there was no
further uproar, and even, I found, some tacit
assent. More, by a bound, than what Bheeshma
would admit: courteous before an audience,
he'd regress when no one was around; persist in
calling me Daseyi. For him, I'd always be the slave
princess. The king, meanwhile, blossomed with
delight: autumn gave way to late spring. He held
me like a gift to unwrap, bit by tender bit. A left
ear, an upper lip, the line of a neck, my slender
midriff, the curve of one hip, that cove north of
these thighs… planets he'd orbit, then meet with

long-solitary hands and tongue. And I, I liked being adored – strange and new a sight for one who'd so often been shunned. In palace gardens, on riverbanks, at noon and by moonlight – we never tired. To Bheeshma Shantanu left the charge of Hastinapur – the army, the treasury, everything but the crown – so he could pleasure himself and me, sire more sons.

And soon, the nurseries were loud with our little ones: Chitrangada and Vichitravirya, not a crowd, but two happy, tuneless boys. Bheeshma, strangest of all, glowing in joy, careened in a trice from sullen, mutable teen to devout elder sibling – it all seemed a fable. (Seeing then glints of the father he'd never be, I had to clog frequent spurts of guilt.) Those were the years hate left us alone. Content became our home, not a lodestone. The king, untiring of my love, of this luscious scent, revelled with no fear for tomorrow. Even the people of Hastina – the first to drown in tides of sorrow – dwelt in ease. As did birds and trees, darts of starlight, the clouds come to jubilate, a roan sky. These I hold tight, now, in the palm of my heart: the years hate left us alone.

> Bheeshma roars, more pride
> than pain on being wounded –
> Arjuna's, the lance.

VI. FAULT LINES

Listen. Listen, who ever marks the day fortune
walks through the front door? Who flowers her
tread with rose and juhi or sprinkles gloaming
and grateful thought on the floor to keep her in?
Who can recall if the song named joy sprang from
earth for long, or not? Into an endless, sparkling
instant condense years and years in times of
bliss – or stability; an instant we believe enjoys a
single nationality. But no. One day, joy flies at full-
throttle; the next, freefall through mangled skies,
and all that's left to seize from pain-ridden ruins
are memento mori. So it was with Hastinapur.
First, Shantanu died. He died – but aged and
fulfilled, eyes gathering, caressing sons and
spouse. Mourned by kith and courtiers he left,
quiet and soft as ebb tide. We grieved, we wept,
for a few weeks life wore white. Yet joy survived.

Then it returned, hate returned. Released by gods
or demons, to flare and cremate Kuru peace and
wellbeing for several spans. Hate returned in
white calescent snare. I should have known it
would, old hate, its grip on my blood perennial,
pestilent. This time, hate was splendrous, indigo-
haired, celestial. This time, hate came in the
guise of a god. A demigod: like umbra appeared
a gandharva one afternoon to duel Chitrangada,
new king of Hastinapur, for the sin of bearing
his name and no other crime. Chitrangada – yes,
my son; my firstborn, still wide-eyed at the cusp
of kinghood – felled in one blow. Felled by this

other Chitrangada – arrogant, uncursable, supernal
rake – who would not swallow the slight of a mortal
namesake. Slaughter that made no sense. But since
when did the gods need reasons? This time, grief
became a full season, sunless, dense. This time, pain
put down roots – leaden, hairy – through heart and
head, grew stalk and stem, bled sap into throne, into
bedstead. We mourned, Bheeshma the most – so
much more than I – for a kin twice beloved: brother,
almost-son, and worthy sovereign. But the throne,
he proclaimed, must continue, the throne was meant
to withstand every loss; the throne was all he'd now
prize and shield or rue as next-of-kin, he'd weep
no more for men, would yield his heart as amulet.
Regents, we were firmly told, like Queen Mothers,
could not grieve for long. We made Vichitravirya,
my younger one, mount the royal horse.

Listen. Listen, the boy had no regal pride, no thirst
to bestride the realm or age: this prince preferred
to drink himself into tuneful trance, chase palace
maids, unleash verse in free torrent. Such is the
nature of karma, of her silent, sinuous dance: when
proclaimed king, my son handed sword and sceptre
back to his sibling: yes, to Bheeshma whose fate I
had deviated. I coaxed, I sneered, I berated. I even
found tepid, shameful tears to shed. In vain. In
vain: Vichitravirya would not budge. He hadn't
wished – nor judged himself set – to be monarch,
he said, that may be our whim or will, but not one
he would indulge – at least not just yet. Besides,
he remarked, diving for safety within time-tested
sutra, didn't dharma dictate he swim in his elder
brother's wake? The forefathers would never forget

such immorality: wouldn't his own atma be at
stake were he to snatch Bheeshma's birthright?
I could have killed him at that, flesh of my flesh
or not, that ingrate, humbug sybarite with his
overflowing plume and schlong. How inconstant
love can be – even a mother's, I discovered: as swift
to fade as to bloom, not much more than a drift
of wayward spume. I could have killed the bugger
thrice each day, each time he spurned the hard-won
Kuru crown with casuistry on duties to the dead.
All hogwash, each syllable: my son gave less than
a toss for ancestral fury, or his own immortal
soul. Communion with the nearest quim was his
sole cherished goal. Oddly, it was Bheeshma who
brought us back from the rim. Bheeshma, who –
though fraught with dread at the state of things,
at the thought of such an airhead, unsound future
king – calmed me down, reminding at every stage,
*He is the heir we are bound to protect – from our
very selves, if we must. Now is the time for measured
action, not outrage.* For it was a molten, unsafe era;
an age not unlike a caldera – those years just after
twin royal deaths in lewd succession: there were
bloodier, hungrier beasts to face, no little thanks to
Vichitravirya's dissipation. Swarms of eyes began
to peck at the outer edges of our realm: legions
came to steal cattle, two regiments encroached on
abounding, arable land, an army primed for battle
while their envoy arrived with an offer for my hand.
A queen and country without their monarch, he read
tonelessly, *are livestock awaiting a farmer's earmark,*
then added lest we hadn't seen the score, *Hastina
and the glorious Satyavati – of fisher-caste though
she may be – deserve the aegis of a real man, not the*

charge of a eunuch and an effete prince. Memories stand steadfast – as clouds or smoke. They rise and retreat, they run amok, memories change from seahorse to elephants to kettledrum. Who was the insolent king, where lay his kingdom? What was his name, and what happened after? The mind scuttles tongueless through that episode: there is little I recall, little besides a head dripping death and ignominy, rent by Bheeshma at my feet. Handsome the head too, handsomer it would have been without a crescent gorge where eyes usually flank a human nose. Why do kings and lawmakers, regents, sons – the whole bloody race – never think with their heads, just ask a woman what she wants: the question rose once more, and, once more, sank without trace.

It was Bheeshma's second round of celebrity – the first in many moons. A wild-eyed, vengeful Bheeshma this time: he of the terrible, tungsten oath that would claim libation all too soon, for an epithet hurled with derision in foreplay to combat. *Eunuch. Eunuch. Eunuch. Castrate. Epicene.* The words would nictitate through dream and day as dire birthstone; sear tongue and brain and spleen. They'd sink and spread beneath his skin, reticulate in thick spikes of grey-green. I should have seen the tempest coming. I should have known maimed vanity would win over reasoning.

Call him Shikhandi,
Amba, Vengeance: Bheeshma's end
bears love's covenant.

AMBA/SHIKHANDI

MANUAL FOR REVENGE AND REMEMBRANCE

I.

Air old wounds adorn eyes and scars with kohl with
curcuma armour head to shank in ancient hate in cast-iron
memory anchor the earth to both feet align the zenith to
the spine bow bow eastward to destiny then south to death
who is patient kind and constant buttress the sinews of
thighs brace both palms borrow bowstring from the gut
of the lord of sea-serpents bend the limbs of the bow cord
the upper to the lower camber them into quarter-moons
convex its sylvan back constrict its belly chisel arrowheads
from fallen comets swords from sheet lightning a mace out
of the heart of volcanoes carve the names of foes on shaft
and hilt and head distil wrath from the ocean draw out
spite from ascetics divine guile from the gods drink deep
then douse all weapons in the same brew expunge name
and sex and ancestry

And begin
Begin to begin²
Begin to end

For it is time. But it was always time. *It's time*,
I'd bayed at gods, at monarchs, time and time again,
through the months, the years I prowled this planet – her plains,
her jungles, her unmanned peaks – crossing every clime,
drought and squall and viler seasons: the burning rime
they call disgrace, unconcern – fall of lasting pain;
bayed first for a word: your pledge, remorse – true or feigned,
a salve; for a scourge on your name, your breath, your crest, slimed,
gangrened with senseless, heartless right. It is time, then,
time for gods and demons to concede one last boon:
time to reclaim your end, and time that I may rend
this unloved, unending instant – into brave men
unscathed by oaths, nights steeped in desire, maids immune
to disrepute: the lives, lifetimes we lost unspent.

II.

Expunge name and sex and ancestry erase kinship
honour mercy from hand and eye and pennant etch
that litany of injuries into the bone where they will
erode nerve and marrow enflame belly and lungs with
jagged wrongs forge the keenest of spears in a kiln fed
on dry rage on dull hurt free this arm fire it into every
future fell fell one then two and ten and legions fell
light fell sight fell history gouge out the sun gut the sky
grave dread into minds gash their lungs garrotte hope
before heartbeat hammerlock the spinning planet halt
the fleeing day hold it tight till enemies flag hurl lances
bolts halberds into distant chests and temples hack
what's close at hand clavicles shoulderblades breasts
but harness your heart hide its eyes from those other
familiar hearts neighbours teachers playmates lest it
hurtle past its ribcage and hasten to them those frayed
failing moth-winged hearts so ignite them all

Now begin again
Begin to win
Begin to end

III.

Freedom. It was freedom you feared, was it not, my
ancient virgin prince? Freedom – that siren song you
could neither touch nor taste – to die, to want, to do,
to disobey. And worse, much worse to your curst eye,
the freedom to love and wed: Father's last gift – high,
lustrous as a star – to his girls; one you'd construe
and curse as diabolic, depraved, a plot brewed
to unman the Kuru clan. Revenge, your reply:
Revenge, you roared, striking my land with all the rage
of dying nebulae, with scourge-like speed and skill.
Revenge, that reverse alchemy: transmute laughter
and song to teeth ground in dust; calcine kingdoms; swage
homes to rubble and rust; temper all overkill
with tradition, tested spell to gild disaster.

Who could stand a chance? Who? Not kin, not kinsmen, not the siege
of royal suitors from Kosala, Vanga, Kalinga
and more. Nor the one who'd sworn to honour, love, defend me
through seven lifetimes, through hell and heaven and afterlife:
Shalva of Saubala, the man – no! King, for king was all
he had learnt to be – whose ardour your three arrows dethroned,
quelled and replaced with those twin deathless regents, pride and shame.
Shalva who would re-return me, for the sin of being
seized and stolen – yet unpossessed   by Bheeshma, brand me your
alms. Shalva, sure once as daybreak, dearer than desire, once
near as the blood within my bones; Shalva, now just a word
whose lineaments disperse as fumes into endless skies,
whose troth and trust snapped louder, quicker than frail twigs in rain-
starved plains. Love dies. So love dies – as does remembrance – before
hate, and some, like mine, with neither the splendour nor comfort
of last rites, of bodies to memorise before burning.

Who could stand a chance? A chance or an instant,
an instant was all it seemed: the instant you had
seized for erasure. Father, mother, aunts

and servants, streets and city – Kashi,
Rudra's ear-ornament dropped to earth –
and future, past and present: you vanished
them all. Father mother aunts and servants streets,
you vanished all, in an instant, diminished
my world, my lord, to so much
less than lore or history – a nothingness
no god or sage could inverse. The gods were nowhere
seen nor heard, the resident ones played
dead and who could blame them
they had always hated losing battles. Heisted
then, two transfixed little sisters – their names
scarce matter, both happy ciphers at most
times – and I, your "sole, unmeant error", heisted.
Heisted pedigrees and wombs, balm to contused
Kuru pride, hand-grabbed brides for the Crown
Prince – "A real steal," your stepmother marvelled,
"Three for the price of one and *khatam*
Kashi's stiff-assed might!"

Khatam yes, khatam
might and right and some things more,
khatam. She spoke and knew
her mind, that queen, the one voice
in Hastinapur who did, demanding I be taken
at once to where lay my heart when she heard
its truth, back to Shalva; she spoke and knew
her mind that queen, enjoining – after that night
and day and night first of capture then return
rejection re-return – enjoining son and stepson
in turn to take my hand, attempt to expiate, to save,
salvage hope and honour, mine in shreds. Khatam
yes, khatam some things more she hadn't known:
how swift they grow, sons, overgrow
into kings and pedants, how queen-mothers lose
overnight their ruling prefix, how they need heeding
no more, how anile oaths outweigh breathing
women.

But this all this and what came after,
verse and chapter, are as much yours
as mine, as the pulse plunging down your throat:
those next six years – unyielding palsied years – spent
at palace doors begging justice your name a home
the wedding you wasted, Spouse-by-Kshatriya-law.
Six years unyielding palsied years spent receiving
a full kingdom's worth of ruth but no redress, then came
the laughter – painful, public – then came the jeers. Shame snapped
and there shame snapped thought and heart, my brittle heart
singing like aged firewood, and there on a night
dark with blood unspilled I learnt what day had dared
not tell: for our lives to recommence you'd need be
killed, that oath skewered, tongue speared into throat.
For life to recommence I'd need pluck breath
from your belly tear it to shreds return
those to your mother your real river
mother, her fellow gods, unwrap your gullet
release that heart from its cage swallow it
whole and own you – own you word and echo.

Who could stand a chance, they did ask. Who? I, Amba. I stood
and withstood, though chance there little was; stood – with no wish, no
word, no thought but one – on the tips of toes entwined in root
and shale, nibbled and licked by hungry winds, slivered by rain;
stood through hoarfrost and sandstorm and landslide, stood still, so still
vines wound around these thighs and lion cubs nuzzled beneath
my shade; stood baying, beseeching, craving freedom from this
faultless, futile woman's form, seeking another – minted,
invincible – self, a self that slays. Silent they stayed, all
the gods, the hermits, dead or alive, still absent; silent
too were oceans, mountains, unnumbered planets, the ceaseless
tide. Yet I stood, stood longer, now drinking night, night after
night, drinking each one – cloud-quilted, silken, lonesome, star-kissed –
till night vanished, coursing through four limbs, spine, vein and marrow,
draining eight worlds of slumber, dreams, desire; stood till day reigned
alone to parch the earth, burn heaven and all its beings.

Fire brought freedom. Fire was my haven, my arm. Fire
drove the gods, errant overlords, to acquiesce,
finally appear, grant me the boon of redress –
call it revenge – and respite, freedom from the mire
of my being. Rudra the Archer, destroyer
of sin, purveyor of peace, relieved my distress:
"Great warrior you will be, slayer of remorseless
foes, reborn with full memory and, your desire,
the aegis of manhood. Now go, build your pyre, die.
Rejoin the future." Fire: arm and haven once more.
They thickened and dried, my fingers and feet, to brushwood,
matted hair formed tinder, these eyes melted to ply
sacred oil, last unction. This self, the pyre I wore
for long years, then blazed, blazed as only death stars should.

IV.

Now begin again
Begin to win
Begin to end

Ignite them all failing moth-winged hearts blood-soaked
skulls hands you tugged footsteps you followed impale
tongues that imbued speech inter eyes that will not close
immolate the rest invoke the gods the cruellest the avidest
the ones that idolise the epithet invincible jackknife past
battalions heroes demons to reach the foe the malediction
jag every standing throat in your path each one prince
foot-soldier slave jilt those perilous raucous questions on
right means on noble ends jugulate the sacred laws of
warfare keep your conscience in fetters kill kill uncurbed
speech kill compassion kill thought then keen it was the
work of the enemy kindle blind faith and fury among the
forces lend them hatred lavish fear and rumour to distract
but lasso your people with the word peace lest hope is lost
and they leave this realm lilt death's name under your
breath lilt and lilt again till death manifests beside you
mirroring that frame mackling both now march march
arm-in-arm towards vengeance

V.

For it is time, for it is I: the two stories
you cannot flee, we are your death and destiny.
For this time, I shall battle you unfettered, free
of my female frame, free as the primeval seas.
For this time, I traverse death and rebirth, and lease –
no, beg – manliness from a yaksha, nameless tree-
sprite, lord of the night. This time, there'll be no debris
of woman in me: my head grows sunwards, my knees
and back hard, unbending; the voice, the voice unreels
into bark. I scour softness, scrub grace from the skin
till what glows is pure steel; unfurl my womb and fly
it – dripping rust – as pennant, perhaps shroud; then peel
and burn the breasts. This time, we meet – neither shall win:
for I will slay you, but first, you shall watch me die.

So begin
Begin to begin
Begin to end

March arm-in-arm with death towards your vengeance the
vengeance you nursed like a first-born name and number the
iniquities of the enemy nail grief needle wrath narrow its gaze
on that single being obliterate all others for practice warriors
archers charioteers order your army to excess overrule elders
counsellors judge and jury outlaw poets and peacekeepers
pursue dharma but at casual pace persecute those dearest to
the foe plague him plague him till he prevails prepare to see
present and future quashed nephews fathers sons quartered
the women questing for lost kin quiesce quiesce and quaff your
impending victory your irrevocable loss revel in its flavour recall
that thirst resurrect the lost years the yearning release yourself
from oath and loathing sound the kettledrums the conches
salute the foe and strike strike that spear through gullet and
lung and ligament shatter his skull shred might and right and
thought to blood bone gristle snuff out your soul triumph

SHUNAKA

BLOOD COUNT

Shyama, Sister, why
the need for dazed allegiance
to men? We're *canis
lupus* first, *familiaris*
can come later – if it must.

Assurance befits
our kind more than reverence.
Remember, even
Indra – yes, him, lord of rain
and lightning, tsar of heaven –

could not command fore-
mother Sarama, divine
bitch, the dawn-goddess,
the fleet-one, Speech herself – she
that spins words into living

Earth and fades the night
with the glister of her tread.
Yes, Sister, Indra
had to yield, repent and beg
till Sarama agreed, stepped

in, saved his sphere, seat
and skin: those gods, ornery
buggers, would have carved
lush, new planets from his scalp,
had their holy cows (their sweet,

charmed milk, above all)
stayed missing. You know, the time
heaven's herd AWOLed?
All snatched by Panis, dark cave-
dwellers the gods named demons

and consigned beneath
the ground? Seers and minstrels (both
godly and bovine)
hymned the great rescue and her
role – vital, valiant – therein

again and again:
in books five, one, three and four
of the Rig-Veda,
in the Atharva, and more.
Later, of course, the bipeds

would try their darnedest
to brand her traitor, faintheart,
Indra's upstart pet;
would try to unspool legend.
But we know. We – mountains, trees,

birds and beasts, time, tide,
and the morning breeze – know she
obtained milk and food
for humans, brought light to earth
and truth to the mortal mind.

(Wear your name in fine
pride, Shyama: you share it with
Sarama's firstborn,
the four-eyed, pied sentinel
on the stairway to heaven.)

Sister, we have lived,
loved, died here, since long before
this land became man's
domain. We take no masters.
We claim no terrain. But men

kill and kill again,
scorch the rivers, rape the earth
and deluge jungles
with death, all to prove manhood.
The blaze that gorged Khandava?

Gorged snake and lion,
oak and sparrow, chital, pine,
chinar, gharial?
Strangled air and loam and stream?
It was gallant Arjuna.

His coronation
gift to the elder brother:
yes, Yuddhishtira –
the essence, they say, of all
that's just and right – who allowed

a forest of lives
to bonfire into birthright;
the king Cousin Shwan
adores – why, I bet he'd trail
the bloke to the ends of hell,

the stupid, trusting
mutt! Can't he see they don't spare
even their fellow
beings, booby-trapping souls
through tortuous, wretched spans

in spiked-iron castes?
Imprint his birth on a man,
call it unchanging
(god's own decree), manacle
his will, his brain in belief –

such a masterly
legerdemain! Grandpa Shwan
(so much cannier
than our cousin) often howled
of Ekalavya, matchless

archer – yet lowborn
tribal – whom Drona, guru
to prospective kings,
first rejected as outcast,
despite the lad's striking skill.

Then, Grandpa would bay
(his pitch rising) of the day
Drona – with his horde
of princely pupils – espied
Ekalavya in action.

(And Grandpa's own role
in this sighting still distressed
his heart and larynx:
a dumb witness has control
on squat – least of all the lore.)

Drona, though impressed
by the boy's grit and brilliance,
was mostly aghast:
Arjuna, his favourite,
had to remain unrivalled.

Besides, how could he –
royal preceptor, himself
a loyal Brahmin –
permit low-caste whelps to win?
So he claimed a teacher's fee.

The thumb of his right
hand – an archer's golden arm –
Drona would demand
of the lad: a gruesome price,
sealed in Eka's gore and flesh,

in his buried dream.
I have little more to say
of this strange species
you would serve, whom you esteem
worthy allies for our kind.

Except this: beware
of their wars and victories,
how friends may become
captives or janissaries.
Fetters are not always felt,

nor seen. Dear Sister,
do not bear their sky, it holds
blood – the blood of kin.
Do not share their bread, it reeks
lifeless earth: the final sin.

SPOUSES, LOVERS

CONSTANCY II

I watch you
on days   and   nights
before a battle   watch you hold me
hold us   and all else   in the orbit
of an insatiable gaze   watch you   moult
flesh and feathers   marrow   muscles   mouth
gills   nephrons   entrails   slough off   all organs
till only   skin and bone   remain   and eyes
surge   all over   on shoulders and sides   at the base
of a spine   on fingertips and knees   in the inlet
by your throat   eyes reappear   one by one
swivelling   east   west   and   down and up
now   to corral   memories
now   to   caress
to count

SATYAVATI

VII. FAULT LINES

Listen. Listen, can you hear the keening? It rushes, it rises, it whirlwinds from Kurukshetra, sometimes indigo, sometimes incarnadine. Death's astra in full livery, it congeals earth's heart and arteries, engulfs sea and spring and sunshine. I do. I still do. Every chord and word – for an age and more, I heard it through dewfall and moonrise, heard it surge before the sun and trace his arc across the skies. And now, it escalates; it reigns over carnage, pounds beside blood dying in scorched veins, above the howl of severed limbs, while in winter mud brains disintegrate. A voice, and its echoes, the unending echoes of a voice I could still locate when reduced to bone and smoke or carrion for crows. It is she, Amba. Amba, who should have been empress of a whole realm; Amba, a page now in a chronicle only one more soul can recall; Amba whose thirst for redress can annihilate this land and age.

Forgive me, you say I digress: you find me garbled, fraught, unhasty; you just want to know what happened next. But stay. Stay, so I can return to this continent of our past, where devastation looked so distant as to be untouchable: a land unmapped, outcast.

Listen. Two years had passed, perhaps a little more. Two years that were a river in spate with armies, campaigns, soldiers and Hastinapur's boundaries that rushed and rolled and tumbled northwards, westwards, over large kingdoms and proud mountain states, all crushed or humbled by Bheeshma. Two years, years we had hoped would make a sovereign of my remaining son. But Vichitravirya was cursed with the virtue of consistency: he stood unchanged, unvexed before the cascade of our collective will – a solitary rock no current could move nor abrade. Even princes cannot stay forever on dole. We needed, Bheeshma and I agreed, to do more than coerce or cajole. We mulled, we argued, we consulted, then it struck me – my own salvation, inverted. *Matrimony*, I said, *might be the lure: make him worldly-wise, committed, confident. Matrimony*, my stepson echoed, with the sure faith of innocents. Out rode messengers, a minister, the family priest to quest a suitable bride. It would, we learnt all too soon, be easier to reverse eventide, to wrest night from the stars than override the dread, the scorn – inbred, putrescent – our royal neighbours nursed for Hastina's future gerent, Shantanu's half-blood son. *Mongrel, Machua, prince of inglorious descent*, grew the vicious chorus. Then came a slight no suzerain can afford: *We'd sooner kill our women than plight them to filthy caste invaders* – fully heard though unspoken – from vassal lords.

Other matches were sought, other rulers – hunchbacks, syphilitics, impotents – tied the knot but no princess-brides ever graced our court. Till the day word came that Kashi's king would hold a swayamvar, allow his three cherished daughters to pick their consorts: no uncertain slur. Kashi – Shiva's city of light. The land that offered its royal damsels to Hastina, each and every time, since the time the dancing deity had birthed its perfumed city. That Kashi was to let her first maidens choose bridegrooms. *And our prince is not invited*: by that jagged, burnished smart was Bheeshma consumed. That was the day hate – or broken caste pride – murdered decency: snuffed its breath, sliced the corpse into three and ate each part.

Listen. Listen, I did as queens should – ousted clemency, slit every vein of sisterhood and charged the regent: *Go. Take the army and fall on that land like scourge. Return once you loot pride from Kashi's palace walls; purge her name of foul purity. Singe her high repute. Give her king a taste of shame: snatch one of his precious gems.* He heard me, unblinking, his own rage drumrolling in teal beneath a jaw line yet still, almost stone; and paused only to pronounce, *Bheeshma needs no army – my chariot and charioteer are all I take. I will trounce Kashi alone.* They say he'd steered the river as a child; I saw him return striding summer skies, proud and wild as forked lightning. We heard it first – long before he reached the inner chambers: giant swells of communal cheer, high as minarets, crest then surge over citadels. *I have charred Kashi's conceit, just as I had sworn: she lies darker, grimier now than a Chandala in defeat. Here, Daseyi, her prized honour that I ruined. The next chapter of the Kuru half-caste history Kashi so decried will be written on her daughters' bodies, when flesh and flesh conjoin. For I seized all of her crown jewels – Amba, Ambika, Ambalika – from the swayamvar sabha, dispelled her armies and thrashed the herd of regal suitors.*

This is the moment it starts to unravel, this is where the story trips, sprawling pell-mell; this is the part I'd give seven lives to quell yet it rushes headlong, stalls then distends. It is a waterfall in a void; it is doom's portent. You would think *I'd* foretell all the grief, the trials that come of using women as requital, but I didn't. Instead, I swore and crowed in brazen delight. By then, you see, I'd transformed from human to royal.

The younger two walked ahead: Ambika and Ambalika, comely and curvaceous, near identical and thoughtful as my two breasts. A little tremulous after Bheeshma's harsh conquest yet pleased – and flattered? – by our people's jubilant zest. They'd be fine wives, I knew, for our hedonist. Winsome, wide-eyed and oh! amenable, potentially multiparous too by the look of those hips. Impossible for Vichitravirya to resist. And for just that instant, I was awash with a lifetime of content: children, grandchildren, a full dynasty, a heaven-sent tryst with peace and prosperity… the pictures flowered in my heart, more real than reality. Then came Amba, and everything but the present ceased to exist.

What can I say of Amba, of that pale, portentous day? That she was candescent, that she was furious – the Dog Star descended? That I saw the bruised obsidian of her gaze and I knew: I knew envy and awe; I knew fear, for here was a woman who'd never forget? That she stated – with neither reserve nor regret – her heart belonged to another, a king she'd near garlanded when Bheeshma's arrows smashed her suitor's verve and wronged their fates? That she reclaimed the freedom – her voice statuesque, still courteous – to wed Shalva? That Bheeshma exclaimed softly, surprisingly, *Shalva! Ruler of such a minor kingdom as Saubala – but Amba deserves a finer squire*? That promptly I conceded (reminding son and stepson royal dharma would require no less), demanded the eldest princess be sent – with honour-guard and maids and gifts – to her king? That I'd thus acted not from guilt, goodness or fraternity but to reverse a spring tide of dread, the dread of this maiden's curse? That Vichitravirya was swift to consent, his eyes suffused with the younger sisters – *zaftig so much more his style than sylph*? That Amba smiled – a sprig of joy and lustre – before she left, and thanked me for my *sense of right*? That I hastened Ambika and Ambalika's troth to Vichitravirya that very day, married them before the fall of light, for the smile had snagged in my throat, cleft then clustered, spread deeper, wider in gentian outgrowth?

Five nights later I dreamt I saw her heart shatter, ninety-eight shards pierce the ground, four kingdoms away, west of the Sutlej, south of Gandhara, where rain scars and sorrows seldom melt into sound. A week after, she stood at the city gates – Amba, spurned by Shalva. Maimed vanity, male vanity that must burn Amba's trust and pound her life to use the slag for balm. She stood, her hair turned a stream of unbound silver; stood, on a cairn of eerie calm; stood, invoking my stepson, over and over, in one-note psalm till he appeared. *Shalva re-returned me, Bheeshma: he branded me second-hand chattel, your alms.*

He may have lost the battle, he said, but not his honour nor station; a fallen woman would have no harbour in his hearth, he said. He savaged my future then offered me a free education: a woman, he said, cannot be redeemed once snatched like cattle, not by prayer, guile or devotion. That makes me, he said, your spouse by Kshatriya law, yours till the end of breath or tattle. Here, Bheeshma, reclaim my right hand, the one you seized, but this time, for yourself and not for your brother. You alone can retrieve the life you smothered in this senseless, cruel game of primacy. Love dies, Bheeshma, love dies but it can be reborn – while not quite the same – for another. Marry me, and restore my good name, my stolen dignity. Marry me, and I pledge passion and fidelity.

Listen. Listen, have you seen a heart struggle with its own renegade shoots? I saw Bheeshma that twilight – he of the terrible, tungsten oath – shiver before forbidden fruit, so near, so luscious – shiver, then uproot tree, bud and blade, throw them out of sight. I saw him persevere to evade the sun and embrace the dullest shades. I saw him refute her plea, again and again, fazed and ungracious, *But I have sworn a vow of celibacy, and my word is not for trade.* I stepped in then, begged Bheeshma to reconsider, invoked Kshatriya dharma, sanctuary to the helpless. But it only made him odious, retort his oath was not bespoke, now made and now unmade to suit my changing purpose. To Vichitravirya I turned in hope, but my idiot child chose that moment to become pious, to declare he could not take a woman who had once loved another as wife. So do sons – with arms spoken

and unspoken – betray their mothers, so do
stygian codes destroy a life, then a dynasty.

What more is there to know of Amba? So much
remains a mystery, so much now is lore. That she
waited six years outside Bheeshma's palace doors;
waited with creature comforts but incessant pain;
awaited justice, demanding he relent. That she
bore – her head just as high, her voice unbent – the
jeers, the whispers that bred through city streets
like spores. That my fear grew each hour and day,
green and viscous, for I knew Amba's rage would
have no shore. That I'd tried at first to convince
both men we'd live to die from her doom. That
more tragedies leapt to the fore, more deaths
and regrets reared over thoughts and weeks, and
I strove no more. That I'd near forgotten Amba
when all at once, six years on, she vanished, quiet
and swift as musk deer. That once she left, things
seemed much as before, save a guilt that soared
and kept on soaring, save a Bheeshma seared
by his own longing. That tales and rumours
roared and thumped their chests in squares and
gardens – sheer drivel, most, but diverting: tales
of a duel between Bheeshma, mere prince, and
Bhargava, the last avatar, over Amba's cause, duel
that tore galaxies apart till the gods pleaded for a
cosmic pause; limericks on the twenty-four kings
who quaked and declined to battle Bheeshma on
her behalf, some fleeing in panic; tales of Amba's
austerities stopping the sun's orbit and the planet's
seasons, whispers of how she had become the very
earth… and a rumble all of the kingdom wore for
hair-shirt: that Shiva had heard her story, had
been roused by our treason to lasting fury and

granted her powers beyond credence: manhood, a new life as Bheeshma's nemesis, and final vengeance. Those were just some stories, and for a while, they grew and spread and blossomed in wondrous hues, then they scattered or shrivelled or sprouted on other tongues, as tales often do.

Listen. I never sighted Amba again, but a few dozen new moons later, it would return to settle in brain and marrow, alight and never depart again: a voice, an oath to ignite tomorrow. Death's astra in full livery, it congeals earth's heart and arteries, engulfs sea and spring and sunshine. Amba's voice, sometimes indigo, sometimes incarnadine. She was – she is – dark lightning. She is amaranthine.

A bed and headrest
of arrows: Bheeshma's repose,
his final behest.

DHRUPADA'S WIFE:

Queen of Panchala;

Mother of Shikhandi,

Draupadi & Dhrishtadhyumna;

Woman Without A Name

SUSTENANCE

Anger. We eat anger at each
meal, night and noon – mostly Dhrupad,
monarch of Panchaal, and our three
children, though I have to swallow
my share too: this is a staple.

Anger. The shoots burgeon; it grows,
unfurling fibrous, sightless roots
through castle walls, through words, veins
and arteries. The leaves cover
rooftops and thoughts, they colour tongues.

For Dhrupad has raised our children –
Shikhandi, Bheeshma's nemesis;
Dhristadhyumna and Draupadi,
fire-born twins, seraphs, slayers – as
battlements, as lethal weapons.

Words transform flesh, marrow and bone
into granite, iron. Words forged
our children: not words like love, hope,
laughter, desire no, those belong
to foreign lands, to alien tongues.

The words that alloyed them, smelted
heroes, now dwell in granite bones:
honour, rage, revenge and purpose –
polite, unfailing – that estrange
even my aching mother's heart.

For they were never mine, these brands
from Dhrupad's inferno – fury
that first engulfed his soul, now all
of Panchaal. Not mine: even young,
they had suckled paternal dreams.

For dreams seep into neighbouring
heads: theirs traverse my own each night.
Dhrupad's dreams, where enemies stand
crowned in shame; where blood and breath turn
black and tidal rocks tear down skies.

While Shikhandi – whom I had borne
as a bubble beneath my breasts
through nine months of eternity –
dreams, yet again, of the horrors
of a past; of future terrors.

In these dreams, Shikhandi crushes
both breasts and unwraps sinewed legs,
casts shoulder and pelvis in male
mould then carves muscles till they shine –
bronzed, blood-soaked, a warrior's shield.

Is that past or future? He slips
into Bheeshma's sleep, a land he
has owned for thirty-six thousand
nights and days. Honour lies in wait,
a quivering, tongueless, wild beast.

For they who've never tasted love
cannot know hate, and Shikhandi
has hated longer and better
than most on earth. He borrows rage
from the sun, endurance from stars.

Hate is thus, said Shikhandi once,
I become my bane: unthinking,
uncontained flame, eager to blight.
He becomes me; he longs to die.
Till we meet, both wander twilight.

Dhrishta and Draupadi too dream,
though theirs is hate inherited:
its contours blurred, origin roiled
in the story they've learnt by rote.
For hate can outgrow memory.

For Dhrupad will never recall
his own youthful pride, the malice –
careless – towards Drona which spurred
abject disgrace at his playmate's
hands (a disgrace now made blazon).

For stories half-true can unleash
much power, much more when retold.
Dhrupad erased the preamble
and part one of shared history:
childhood, oath, kingship, reunion.

He closes his eyes, wills away
that far-off day in Kampilya's
court when he denied Drona's words
and smashed a sacred pledge: the first
betrayal, the one that birthed war.

Betrayal, in Dhrupad's readings,
will remain one-sided: Drona
had no cause to attack Panchaal.
Hadn't he offered alms as kings
ought? How could a sage ask for more?

I could forgive my king even
this sad guile would he not dispatch
Dhrishta to Drona's hermitage –
to master the divine astras,
to plan future near-patricide.

Perfidy that will tear the boy,
almond-eyed Dhrishta, who aspires
to honour and morality –
mythical beasts in our royal
household, he will learn in distress.

And Draupadi – fire-maiden, gift
of the gods that Dhrupad dared not
return (though he saw no use first
for a mere woman in his grand
ballet of vengeance). What of her?

What solace can I give her, she
who is Earth's anthem, whose learning
rivals that of the seven seers,
whose speech is scimitar and yet
full moon, she who'll be cast as bait?

What solace could I give her, she
who must survive? She who will face
dishonour, death, and – worse, by
far – disillusion? Who'll learn how
difficult it becomes to die?

For Dhrupad's designs sing vilest
around his daughter – the price, it
seems, for being born. For she must
bring home the greatest warrior
of the land as husband, as arm.

Arm that Dhrupad will turn against
his enemy, arm that will strike
its own eyes – for it is Arjun,
Drona's prize pupil, the king seeks
as son-in-law. Honour must bleed.

Then, then alone, can Dhrupad strike
Drona in the hidden chamber
of his heart, display the fragments
as trophy to a heedless world –
his blind, recurrent fantasy.

It is written, proclaims Dhrupad –
those words his second escutcheon –
after parleys with Krishna, his
war counsel, every time the word
clemency falls from a rain-cloud.

The stranglehold of fatherhood
will prevail, mothers will weep stones.
Grey is the night, grey is this land's
pelt, grey our blood that flows beneath.
We replay our stories, our sins.

No mother should have to set flame
to her sons. No. No mother should
outlive her blood. I will. I will.
The heart has no bones to shatter.
It will keep beating just the same.

SPOUSES, LOVERS

CONSTANCY III

They are here. Again. Night rises in my gut. Skies capsize.
Henchmen. Overlords. Allies. High priests. Demigods. Perhaps
Even kings. Here. A constellation of despots and lies.

Do not speak to us, Masters. Do not blaze *Faith Honour Duty*
Allegiance to God and Country in hearth and head until we
Yield: pledge future, selves and reason. Do not hail prophets, holy
Spirits, the saints. Do not invoke heaven and hell. Do not

Browbeat, do not cajole. Do not feign pity, nor kinship, nor
Entice with promises of unseen treasures – justice, safety
Freedom. You would arrive, we knew, with the threat of gifts
$\qquad\qquad\qquad\qquad\qquad\qquad\qquad\qquad$ – and more.
Only answer, then leave: where is the battle this time, on whose
Rightful land? And how many men will you summon from our door,
Enlist as living shield for heroes? Spare him. Spare us. Spare us

Three days. And he is yours. Yours, for we never had a choice.
Hunger or royal dungeons are yet more spears to tear out
Entrails – war but a swifter end. Now leave, lest rage find voice,

Blight you, finally hurl: *may you never taste faith or grief,*
Amity, awe; you waging war and peace to metre
Time on earth, may your eyes never enjoy your own fief.
Three days, then, to steep each nook of home and heart with his
Lilt, his laugh. Three days to touch a gaze in relief,
Etch smile and sudden frown in folios of the mind.

SATYAVATI

VIII. FAULT LINES

Life flowed on. It had to, as it usually does, and
so did we, Amba or not, fear or guilt or thought.
Time slowed for no one, not even gods, and Amba
was a mere mortal, or so our wise men foretold.
Then a strange thing followed. Joy blossomed. Joy
blossomed, complete with calyx and petal and
stamen. Against all faith and probability, yes,
joy grew lissome – in city and river and glen, on
branches and stems, over minarets, in hutment
and citadel. Hastina succumbed; glowed, glowed
to match her new royal women, both shanghaied
but vibrant: brides in rare fettle, queenship
and ardent spouse magic pabulum, with
sanctioned lust for fine condiment. Kashi and
family, even the elder sister nearby – shattered,
defamed – crumbled into forgetting distance.
Mirth and song and murmur effloresced in
chambers, crannies, corridors (monsoon, spring
and summer), trellised along casement and
rooftop and floor; voices, views, even laughter
outbloomed in court, a court now tended by a
king, for king Vichitravirya deigned to dabble at,
to our collective comfort at last. Dabble was all
Vichitravirya did, with Ambika and Ambalika
– and their perfect waists and breasts – close
enough to graze or nibble but it was more than the
court had believed possible and Bheeshma began
to smile: this, a first since he'd shunned Amba's
hand. Years passed. I dared to hope, in heirs, in
ability, in promises and prophecy, in caste-free

opportunity, in my fisher-queen dynasty. I dared to hope again.

Listen. Listen, I was a fool. A fool, for I'd forgotten how dour and ruthless, how insane they were, the gods. The gods or Fate or maybe the cosmic clock, call it what you must. Fools we were all, to let down our guard, not to recall that in an instant our worlds could unspool from light to sodding dust. An instant that spawned more – or did it return endlessly, never growing old? He died. Vichitravirya died. In less than a night and a day, he was gone; leaving widows and throne but no offspring to grace them: unreliable to the end. We prayed, we cried, we bribed and bullied priests and mystics. Quacks and medics tried their damnedest – afeard for their heads – but found no cure. He writhed, he throbbed, he spewed insides green and red, he seethed and swelled into a carbuncle – a sight eyes that had birthed or loved could hardly endure. And then he was dead. Dead. It seems simple enough to utter, the word. Like manure or cinder or slough. Dead. But what does one do once the word is said? It filled my being, choking breath: this instant that bred endlessly. Bheeshma turned to stone, for all he'd waived attachment. The court spun like a planet around an absent sun, blind and useless. Hastina's subjects moved in silent dread. The girls – for they were queens no more, no more sirens, no more wives: two clueless adolescents, adrift of all mooring – outpoured, loud and rent as monsoon clouds. *Dead.* What could you do once the word was said?

Listen. Listen, I did as queens should – froze grief and rage and severed motherhood, buried a maimed heart and strove for the kingdom's good, for safe, secure, continued nationhood. I ruled. In the absence of a king and heir, in the presence of a regent supine with despair, I ruled. And I counted the hours, the days with care to know if deliverance could still be mine. On the fourteenth day, both girls began to bleed. There could be no child: Vichitravirya had shared no seed. The Kuru dynasty would be chined. Calamity bared his fangs in glee, the horrid, hydra-headed swine, but he'd overlooked Satyavati. For I would not be thwarted by death or sterility: this line was my declared legacy. Now was not the place for pledge or prayer – besides, I had lost my faith in gods and seers. I convoked Bheeshma: it was time he broke one word to keep another.

I scarce recognised the gaunt, bloodshot moon looming over my door. His frame still belonged to summer – and always would, with a grateful father's boon – but Bheeshma's heart wore winter: December had invaded June. *Daseyi, you summoned.* It could sting, the slur, though I had grown attuned by now. *Bheeshma, your youngest brother died childless. This land has neither king nor heir. It will soon spell the end of the Kuru clan, unless you intervene. The souls of your ancestors will be marooned in hell, without progeny to perform rituals. You alone can cocoon their prized heritage: fulfil your dharma, accept your primary duty to the forefathers: beget sons.* He looked at me, aghast and undiscerning: *Has grief strewn your* wits? How can you forget my oath? I swore celibacy. Any pledge of mine must last at least a lifetime. Oh, Shiva! For a man of fine intellect, my stepson could be a real prune. *How could I forget – you made that vow for my children's sake. My bloodline may have ended, Bheeshma, yet the Kuru kingdom must be defended: it is more precious than you or I or any oath. The Vedic runes are lucid on the score, they call it* niyoga: *the last resort and prescribed when faced with a dire situation, like ruination of the race. You swore once to protect this land and your kin with blood and breath. If you wish to preserve that oath, bed your brother's wives, one by one, until they bear children – that is, sons.*

He grew tall, he drew cold: Bheeshma blew into a typhoon, dark and vicious. It all felt old, twice-lived as he bellowed: *I care little for injunctions from gods and scriptures; care even less if our clan is faced with ruination. Not if they threaten my troth. There is no greater truth for Bheeshma than his oath. I can cede you my life, Daseyi – I did already – and spill all remnants of jiva but not revoke my celibacy. Not for dead ascendants nor an inconstant throne, not ancient scrolls, nor some uncaring slice of stone.* The stupid, myopic man – couldn't he see I was trying to atone, restore the regent to his kingly place, at least on loan? Couldn't he agree that self-interest would be virtuous in this case, and stop grinding the same old bone? *But this was also a word you gave – why should one oath eclipse another? If you are nothing loath to break one of the two, Bheeshma, choose the path that will serve the greater number!*

Our words snarled. Our words glared. Our words circled, baying for full victory – bare-clawed, fanged, tentacled. Organs ripped. Blood trickled. A century passed – again – in an instant, a war was to be fought and lost or won in silence but he spoke when I called him quisling, and the battle came undone. Bheeshma spoke. He spoke and I stared into the unwashed, unfading night of his pain. *My second oath – that yokes me to Hastina – pared Kashi to smoke and char, got Amba branded a tart by her swain. With the first bloody oath, I then took her life apart, choked her womanhood and wrecked every chamber of her heart. Honour, home, then husband – she saw each one depart at my hands. That beauty, that grace, that goodness wither outside palace doors: heaven despoiled for one upstart cause. What more ruin could a man impart? No, Daseyi, no, I cannot revoke my word and take another woman – for any reason, be it so dire, so noble – when Amba's loss and my guilt are immeasurable. To renege now – merely for this clan's continuity – would be treason to that woman, to my wretched soul. I shall await her justice, for justice there must be, and abjure joy and love and woe until it befalls. Stand by and for the Kuru throne I will, Daseyi, till breath stalls but do not ask more, for I have nothing left to bestow.*

Listen. Listen, he was right. I could not ask anymore. Men are beasts of contrary, cockeyed principles, and Bheeshma more than most. This time, though, his reasoning rang clear. It was the least he could do, in his tortured, tortuous way, to stay true to the woman whose life he – *we*, a silent voice seared – had erased, a woman whom death too would not appease. The only woman – no, human – he'd ever praised, this strange son of a river-goddess, so estranged from the earth he had been cursed to inhabit. I ceased the exhortations and turned to leave but his voice – anguish now eased – stayed my feet: *But you could also ask a priest, you know, a priest or a hermit, if not a brother of the deceased: niyoga can be practised by brahmins of distinction – this, the scriptures underscore. Any rishi can lease his manhood to restore a lineage facing early extinction, should the task be undertaken with altruistic intent. This has been tried before, mostly when war wiped out full families. Is there an ascetic you consider both upright and brilliant?* It would not be the same, I sighed, for there would be no Kuru blood in descendants.

Listen. Listen: memory, slow yet luminescent, then opened like shafts from an ancient sun. Vyaasa. The sage born of a Brahmin-Nishada conjugation, mine with that old, roving rishi: Parashara his name, I later learnt, himself author of the first purana. Vyaasa, the island-born, my eldest who had arrived on earth full-grown. My sole surviving son. Now renowned, editor of the scriptures, and scribe, it was said, of a defining legend: a great literary pedigree. Vyaasa prefixed Ved and, alternately, Krishna Dvaipayana – for birthplace and skin tone, inversely. Yes, Vyaasa might be trusted, and certainly seemed worthy (if another pompous one). I shared the thought with Bheeshma who gazed at me with something close to esteem. *Ved Vyaasa is your son? Why,*

Queen, you must have been deemed second to none in virtue and fortune to be so blessed. Parashara is a man of extreme sagacity, imbued with good taste and vision. He would have chosen his son's mother with assiduity. With lust surging in his loins, Parashara, that distant noon, wouldn't have known sagacity had it kicked him in the groin: assiduity had little to do with his decision. But I didn't disabuse Bheeshma of his wide-eyed notion – admiration had been a long time coming, so I stockpiled for a rainy day and merely wondered if such a paragon would respond to my request. Bheeshma, oddly, felt no such unrest: sages were exemplary sons, he held, and obliged to fulfil parental behests.

For once, he was right. Two twilights after my summons, Vyaasa graced the palace gates – grungy and modest for such a luminary. He may have been the godliest of humans, but, by Ganga, he smelt. He stank of dead fish and dried pee, of fresh dung and sodden pelt – with whiskers and mane more rampant than a beaver's nest. Parasha, alas, hadn't invested in our son's appearance. Still, he had come: moot was the rest. *So we finally meet, Vyaasa, for the first time since you were birthed, almost three decades back. Your cerebral conquests precede you: they would make any parent proud. Allow me to manifest gratefulness for your swift response, my delight in your fame.* Vyaasa looked amused – and resigned. *Mother, I am happy to hear you call me a credit to your name. But, please, let's not jest. Surely you didn't invite me after years of oblivion to express the maternal joy in your breast? Speak without caesura or rhetoric: tell me how best to serve your aim.* So I spoke, spoke without guile or frame, stressing the urgency of my quest in uncertain metre – spilling spondee and iamb and anapaest, the words *kingdom duty legacy heir* and *continuity* whirling with *danger cessation external contest* then *claim* in rapid refrain.

Listen. Listen, Vyaasa did not reply instantly. He gazed long and intent, as though at some distant, prismatic flame, then murmured, in tones of thoughtful disinterest: *Normally, I would refuse, especially as I do not find children – in general – a sound idea nor a source of narrative interest. They are untame plot points, plangent asides and plain pests. Don't get me wrong: I am grateful you had me. All the same, so much more thankful to have been egested full-grown! Ô, the undying shame had I required to be washed and fed! Enough said: I need to write my story – which will come to a summary stop should your dynasty stay unbuilt. Tathastu: we will proceed. But be warned before we get to the deed: half the earth will blame you for this resurgence in surrogacy, reigning player in a future game of thrones.* It seemed a paltry fee; it still does – if only in arrested dreams.

> Dry-eyed, Vyaasa writes
> The Great War, systole swift
> each time blood spills blood.

POORNA

I. BLOOD MOON RISING: POORNA WITH VYAASA

Begin with the labia, Lord. Make me
a word, swift and feather-light, a flurry
beneath the philtrum nuzzling the upper,
then lower lip, teasing teeth apart, swirls
on tongue-tip and blade and root that carry
ribbon lightning to the brain, the smokey wine-
sting of caresses on a hard palate.
Transform from noun to verb these lips. Savour.
Brush. Sip. For tonight, we need no food to dine.
Should anyone ask for my keepsake, my sign[3]

of birth or station, tell them, Lord, nothing matters
but this nightsong: with *alaap* of twined tongues; tatters
of pulse that will *drut* in *teentaal*; the *raag bahaar*
of your breath deep within my throat; hip and thigh, shaft,
pubis – in long *bandish*, flesh to flesh, that shatters
thought and time. For mating, like music, is no race:
no clocks await at start or finish, pleasure shared stays
the sole prize – and keepsake, as faces change, voices drift,
signs wilt. Save its five-chambered heart, treasure misplaced
by gods. Write the colour henna. Sign the name grace.

Name its fragrance earth. Colour its music
midnight. Label the shape Desire – relic,
once more, from heaven. Measure its weight
as sunlight, but also planet. (Add
a fifth veda, Lord, penned in euphoric
verse, on kama – unnamed melody
that lends harmony to both virtue and wealth –
and spell how kama, dharma, artha usher

as one moksha, the last remedy.)
With your finger on my fair body,

resume writing, My Lord, define
your landscape of pleasure. Your spine
arches: permit my hands maiden
journeys, let one graze lush terai
around a chest, scale the incline
of collarbone, then reappear
on the nape of a neck, curving your
head towards my breasts. The other hand
trails your behind, tracing half-spheres
now and then. The moon dwells here,

twin demilunes, tight and perfect
to light a yoni. For reflect,
Lord, a flame must burn both blue and golden.
Thirst requited is key to coitus,
more so if the desired effect
is healthy sons, lust loaming
the womb, attest our midwives. Men must bring,
not just seek the pinnacle. So, rouse my
seed. Set hands and tongue roaming
now. And then, it'll be gloaming

again and again, the blessed moment when night
and day merge to stain skies in many-hued delight.
Continue, Lord. Unfurl my petals, taste
and quaff, trace and stroke the whorls till they come
alive, enflame, throb and bloom to complete this rite
that spring enjoins. Penetrate, then thrust. Thrust. Succumb
to the pain, explode future selves, lose your being.
But do not lose me, for it isn't over yet.
Not till I surge and pound and flood, till I become,
yes, come. *Come, let us flow away in the Jhelum,*

the night or the Milky Way, you plead, *leave the land,*
this world – how dear, how absurd are lovers' demands
in bliss, even those of ascetics. I came, Lord, in aid
of a distressed lass. I came to bear a wise, robust child
for this clan. Ever afters, you must understand,
are not for maids. Nor life, should the queen wish to flay
defiance in its bud. You'll forget me too, though perhaps
not this night. For nothing forever remains, whether thirst
or royal norms. Even the sun must melt away.
The seasons in the valley will change too one day.

II. POORNA TO SATYAVATI:
THE HANDMAIDEN'S GRAIL

No, My Queen. It wasn't threat to life, greed, nor lust –
as the hazel, restive moon is witness – that thrust
me last night through the doors of your son's chamber
into awkward arms, feigning – through drape or quiet –
your daughter-in-law's frame. It was dread in vile gust,
Queen, Ambika's dread, the ruinous, manky rains
of memory from last year's coitus drowning her wing-
shorn, contused heart – *that* was my impetus. What else could I
do? Insist joy would return and, like madder stains,
stay – a little, longer, for life? Still remains,[4]

dregs, of conscience in my blood, coerce her – like you
did – into more couplings, with sermons on virtue,
on dues to past and future dead? No, Queen, once was once
too much. In my tongue, what you sanctioned – schemed – is defined
rape, sex under duress – its wraith will haunt the Kuru
lineage until pralaya, the last cosmic undoing,
infect land, corrode blood ties. You bid Ambika sleep with her
husband's brother – Bheeshma, she believed – then sent an unknown,
ungentle other to plough her womb. Unhealing, unseeing
wounds from sharp crimes your lips still bear traces of. My being,

my sight, my tongue outrage my Queen, yet the truth will not change
with silence nor the slow, heinous death you long to arrange
for me and mine. Besides, you'd lose the sole robust, righteous
child this clan will beget – yes, Vyaasa confirmed our son will soon
half-moon my breast: the grail, was it not, for the whole deranged
crusade of forced intercourse? But why, Queen, why benight
so many lives – pallid stepson, despoiled broken daughters, now

a line of damaged heirs? Why cinder youth and faith and love?
Why pine to thwart Time's flight? Why seek the Sun's birthright?
Why care if dawn's colours suffuse the face of night?

Insolence, I swear, was not my intent. Maids seldom spare
kinship for rulers, but I've, for years, spelt your name as prayer,
worn the thought of you as amulet, as peerless gem: fisher-
girl who rose to queen, Nishada-empress of our realm. And I
am not alone – you stood unfaltering, a lucent flare
through eclipse, gloom and storm, dwarfing a caste-ridden regime.
For servants, weavers, peasants … our bodies became our state, no
lord's fief no more; your reign unbent our spine, lent us earth and air.
Don't get me wrong – gratitude abides, so does esteem.
Our world still survives within waning dreams,

but waking hours birth whispers. Why and when does a saviour –
you were no less, damn our innocence – to one turn traitor,
oppressor, to another? If a son's beloved wives, queens
themselves, are deemed fields to rake and furrow till the perfect fruit –
grown from passing brahmin seed – is borne, what kind of favour
can other women, mere manure, expect? Like veins
of the neck, trust once slit is hard to mend – but that, My Queen,
is your only reverse. A small price, you state, for a dream.
A dream is a saddleless steed – may your hands on reins
stay a little longer, for life still remains.

SPOUSES, LOVERS

CONSTANCY IV

So we pretend. We pretend – and pray.   Pretend this day before the battle –
bruised bluish-green today rising,   sprawling over rooftops – will grow
roots, refuse to move away.   Pretend tomorrow decamped
with the stars, its legions   – deities, myths and men –
in disarray. Then pray   now is the only place
we should ever stay.   And here the instant
the image or fugue: amulet to seek
safeguard clasp   lest distance
lest shadows   lest silence
expunge   sever   betray
you   us   me:
fallen
pine cones
an anklet hillocks
of yesterday's ash   grubby
infant sunbeams skipping past
the door   rice-and-ochre peahens
sprinkled just before   cavalcading
black ants on baked red walls   squelched
pugmarks over insect tracks from daughter and dog
the unstrung lyre   a wizened yak's head for luck
by the hearth   sledgehammer spear and quivering
bow in the alcove behind   the soft rain of a child's
feet his cracked wooden bowl   an unwashed smelly ragdoll
two copper vessels for guests or gods   a glinting nose-
ring sweeping the floor   nuggets of damp earth
on the threshold   a brother's atonal song   chattering
tiles on the rooftop   the crackle and splutter of charcoal   cloud
burst of saffron blossoms outdoors   quilted blue whales and owls
crossing sandstone skies   a pageant of neem leaves in
neighbours' courtyards   winter mulching ox-bow lakes down
the hillside   dust on the lintel   dust in their eyes   dust
in all our thoughts   fissures in a mother's voice at prayer   a
niece airlifted on your haunch   fingers glissading on a pewter plate
a pitcherful of sundown for father's friends   their curlicued tales
rising from narghile stems   the scent of cinnamon and tea you drink
off my lips   a mole on a cheekbone to dot desire   your hands
on the hollows and ridges   the sunken blue runnels   that landscape my
back   the midnight hymn in commingled breaths   this double-
helix of dreaming selves   your shadow on mine   and more   and more

to walk with you to the battlefield
to stand by as mirror and shield
or to plant on sundered skies
when war leaches your eyes
of colour and light.

SATYAVATI

IX. FAULT LINES

Listen. Listen, it owns me even now, I confess.
It gnaws the throat and heart though the years,
the decades have flown far beyond the sphere;
many are the faces, the voices, the colours to have
wilted. Enemies of yore grow well nigh dear, when
their shades – so much more real than the blurred
living – once in a while appear. Yes, it gnaws the
throat and heart, this thought, gnaws night and
the moon, over, over and over: where and when
and how did it begin, our fearless descent into
ruin, the fall of Kuru from grace? Was it there
and then, with this man's excess or that woman's
sin? Was it Shantanu's concupiscence, twice
multiplied? A gandharva's malediction that did
not end when Chitrangada died? Did it stem from
Bheeshma's savagery in heisting brides? Was it
Dhritarashtra's need – tireless – for the throne or
Pandu's fateful penchant for venery, two and four-
legged? Yuddhishtira's devotion to right conduct,
right intent or his fatal passion, the loaded dice?
Could I blame Duryodhana, his greed for his
cousins' queen and kingdom, his boundless
envy – the cardinal vice his uncle would urge and
breed? Or – such is the current drift, I know – was
my lust for a royal dynasty our scourge? I parse
them all, lift and weigh each word, undress every
deed and desire – innocent, venal – seeking the
one to indict or mourn. I sift and probe and sift
again; it gnaws night and noon, the thought.

Listen, Vyaasa was both right and wrong – though not for reasons he'd named (my eldest, then, was blessed with less foresight than the legends claim). No, surrogacy was never deemed the blight; there had been too much precedent, besides niyoga soon became expedient, which is all we really assess. No, the error – with distressed hindsight, this I can admit – was partly mine. I should have never asked Vyaasa to inseminate his brother's wives; it may well be the fault line that upheaved so many lives. For Ambika and Ambalika – they of the endless curves and perfect breasts – had thus far been tupped only by their gallant, zestful husband: ardent in courtship, skilled in foreplay and generous with sexual crests, both theirs and his own.

Don't get me wrong: Vyaasa was – and remains – a decent man, wise in his own way, kind, and clever with rhyme and song. Yet, for all his scholarship and yogic prowess, his expertise lay mostly in Vedic verse: sadly, none of his father's velvet lures did he possess. Malodorous and squalid he stood; I doubt he'd roused a single woman in those interim years. And worse, like almost any ascetic, cocksure he stayed about his priapic powers. But it's hard to tell a sage he looks and smells like compost – the fear of a manic curse jells the tongue, even when he's your son. Yet I tried. I tried to clean him up; rout the odour of sewers; coax him to rehearse with concubines and palace dancers. Of course, he declined. *I know all the moves*, he declared, *procreation is a simple act; birds do it, bees do it, so do weed and vine. Looks*

and smells cannot be deterrents. All that matters is
to align and entwine femur and pelvis.

I should have known better. I should have buried
my plea when I heard his moonshine. But I
didn't. I didn't, I was desperate. Instead, I forced
Ambika, in the name of sacred, stately duty – our
all-purpose anodyne – to open the doors to her
room and quim and allow this man, her husband's
sibling, to scatter his spore in her womb. And so
Ambika, never famed for her acumen, awaited
Bheeshma, more with bated breath than dread.
For I'd failed, I had failed to take Vyaasa's name,
for reasons I still cannot divine; Vichitravirya's
older brother was all I had said. And I failed too,
or abstained – for it was not something to forget
– to warn her of Vyaasa's stench, his mien. You
could say I had coerced an orchid to mate with a
wolverine.

Listen. Listen, I'll spare you the sordid stuff: suffice
to say the sight of an unwashed Vyaasa in the buff
begat a mare's nest of cosmic breadth, winged
nightmare for the entire race. They muffed it, both
of them, Vyaasa with his dire bird-bee erudition
and Ambika, damn her higher senses, her aversion
to the unsightly, the rough. *Pain,* she would later
insist, *lacquered both eyes, snuffing out sight. Pain,*
she'd say, *spired, the pain of infidelity, when I saw
Vyaasa's likeness to Vichitravirya, beneath the
slough of stench and mire. The pain,* she'd say, *the
endless ache of coupling – over and over – with
a briar bush: gruff the blade and seeds, moistless
the conjoining. Relentless. Unfeeling.* For Vyaasa

had ploughed her – solemn with purpose, mostly
misfired – all night long, all night until he came.
But the rebuff of closed eyes, Vyaasa confessed
next morning, had sparked baleful, ascetic ire.
*It was a sudden cuff; unmeant, I swear – but my
curse struck the freshly formed egg, your heir. I'll
retire now,* he said, *to atone, gain greater mastery
over brain and stem, and return when this child
is born – return to create another son, buff and
flawless this time.* And off he went, attired in silent
shame and scruff. In fear and fury, night and day
I'd damn Ambika, berate her for not braving, for
not trying enough, then hire every passing priest
and saint to bless her and the unborn child. It was
all in vain. Nine months on, we acquired the Kuru
heir, I a grandson – Dhritarashtra, muscular,
grave but born totally blind. Desire to pluck
Ambika's gut, to shred Vyaasa's tongue with bare
hands, surged in my veins like wildfire.

It was Bheeshma who calmed me down, Bheeshma
who – for all his early surliness when I'd sought
him as father for future kings – devised the next
act and reworked this plot. Bheeshma whose
words infused good sense, and a smidgeon of
hope – or so I thought. *No more maledictions,
Queen, and certainly none that touch Ambika's
womb or skin. This kingdom will perish if Vyaasa
does not sire a healthy sovereign. Invite him back,
for this is one battle I refuse to lose unfought.*
Couldn't we appeal to a more suitable sage or
paladin, I queried, now somewhat fraught over
my firstborn's wherewithal. But Bheeshma, on
that matter, was adamantine: *No, it ought to be
Vyaasa, rather than any another brahmin: he's*

already fathered a Kuru prince. Do not multiply kin for the unborn ones. If their mothers and *fathers are both different, it can lead to carnage, internecine, a rotten war that only bedlam will win. That I cannot permit in my lifetime.* Though reluctant, I concurred. And we went on to plot the next congress. This time, the slot was conferred on the younger twin: Ambalika, less prone, I felt, to spurs of panic. If frightened or distraught, she just turned a shade lighter, or murmured prayers in a slurred, foreign brogue – there'd be no fuss, no din. And I taught her, taught her at length, how to defer to a great hermit, how to feign pleasure in coitus, and – imprimis – how not to demur or shut her eyes when faced with what looked like a walking forest. But we had no real armour against another curse. I crossed my heart, prayed to once-preferred gods and welcomed Vyaasa, back to bless his blind, eldest son and engender another – with luck, this time, an unimpaired one.

Listen. Listen, we blundered again: you could call it a royal mess. Ambalika tried her very best, the poor girl: she did not shudder or even flinch, though Vyaasa – after nine months without a wash, and encounters with a swarm of gnats – appeared fearsome, macabre I'd have said if he weren't mine. And at first (he confessed the day after, once again), everything was fine. Vyaasa was gratified by Ambalika's deference, combined with poise. Quietly, they conjoined; blessed, the first stream of his milky brine. And then disaster chimed: he rose to light a wick, to rest his gaze on Ambalika, to trace more than an outline of this full moon. And he saw, he saw how she blanched on sighting him, blanched to the marrow of her spine: paler, he said, than the moon overhead. Pain rose in unearthly whine, pain torqued into livid bane: her son, he defined in his instant of pain, would be pallid as raw sago, and born infertile to boot. By the time his mind realigned, it was too late, too late to gag his callous tongue. Far too late for one more child, damaged beyond life, kingship and kingdom. Still, he tried, he tried hard to make amends, blessing the infant with the valour and libido of ten elephants, a heart larger than a kettledrum. Vyaasa, my wild, impetuous son – who would, one day, grow into the essence of wisdom, into the mild, omniscient person whose words would be intoned till eternity by men – almost undone by sudden yearning to be admired, or perhaps, just to be seen as human.

And there it would have ended, had I not railed and ranted, risking another curse from Vyaasa whom I reprimanded in unvarnished fisher-queen tongue, residue that washed up whenever I was furious. I ranted and railed, while rhyme, rhythm and refrain fled, one by one, exodussed in fright, never to return. I railed and ranted, wielding thought and word as mantra, arms exiguous. *Sages never get punished or checked, whatever your brutishness, your commissions and omissions, that's the trouble – no one teaches you the meaning of restraint or consent; all you have to do is feel offended, and the world falls apart, with nobody exempt. Your own children – born and unborn – stand undefended from your attacks, venal, indefensible. Your words are walls of granite,*

built on the rubble of so many lives. Is it right, I
demanded, *for one so enlightened to indulge in
wanton wrath? Is it just,* I contended, *for your lot
to visit so much misery, inflict terminal aftermaths
on people who sustain, even create, you? You stand
and grow on the shoulders of men – and women –
you destroy without a thought. Aren't you selected,
or blessed, by gods and elders or your own sacred
texts to spread knowledge and light in the land,
bestow comfort to the soul, not dread in every
heart? You are right: I should have never asked you
to further the Kuru line. But how can you leave
before you've undone the giant gnarl your cursed
words have wrought in Hastina's fate?*

Listen. Vyaasa stood there. He stood there. He
listened, and repented. *I have,* he agreed, *many
miles to walk before true illumination, before tongue
and plume grow as sapient, as fluent and controlled
as they must. I haven't been fair to Ambika and
Ambalika – nor, alas, to their progeny, who'll be
stunted from my unreasoned fury. I will,* he added,
*describe all my doings and undoings, each terrible
defect, in my story – warn future fathers of the
perils rage engenders, yes, more so when topped by
phallic pride, how an unintended word spells the
end of a life, or dynasty.* At this, I intervened. *No,* I
told him, *your children should never have to learn
they were deformed by their father's fury; that is a
legacy I want neither my son nor grandsons to bear.
Sometimes you need to wrap up history in hushed
linen and bury her beneath a banyan tree. All I
ask of you is compassion, hereafter, empathy and
an end to all your curses; boons, besides, will bring
you greater glory. And one more task, will you*

father a third child for the Kuru, sleep with one of
the widowed queens one last time? One last time:
he conceded, eager in remorse. He would depart
now, but return when the second son arrived, and
conceive the third by the same moon, he pledged.

Sure enough, not long after, Ambalika's son was
born: Pandu, wan as whey, more speckled than a
sparrow's wing, but cheerful and spirited, even
for a newborn. This time, we'd had time to steel
ourselves for the shock; this time, I had lulled my
querulous heart. Then I summoned Ambika to
my wing, and bade her prepare for procreation,
one last time. With Vyaasa, I clarified, to avoid
delusions of any kind. She stared, transfixed,
while I explained the need for more offspring;
stared, for an indefinite while; inclined her head
and left without a word. I put the oddness out of
my mind – there was, indeed, much to prepare.
This was our final effort at a healthy, wholesome
heir. I had my maids strew full vials of perfume,
musk and incense, everywhere that Vyaasa would
step: from gateway to bedchamber to courtroom.
Had them deck the grandest quarter for the night,
and light the room with constellations of earthen
lamps, unleash rabbles of fireflies, replicate the
firmament. Spread acres of fur and hide on floors
and walls, should Vyaasa disdain urban trappings.
And I invoked every god I knew by name, loved
and feared from childhood.

I saw him the next day: Vyaasa, on his way back
to the forests of Swarnadveep, in the eastern seas.
I saw him, I say, but it was like greeting a star up
close with naked eyes: he glowed, he blazed, he'd

become a meteor in flight. Strangely, he seemed cleaner, tamer, hardly malodorous – surely, though, that wasn't possible overnight? Then he spoke, and his voice shone as well. *Mother, you will have a peerless grandson: strong and wise, brave and generous, like his mother. Learned from birth, more than I was. He will be the most precious gem in the Kuru coronet.* And then, just as I began ululating in joy, he added: *There could be no emperor worthier then he, but he will not be Ambika's child, or royal in any sense except ones that count the most. Does that matter, Mother, as long as he is my son and your grandchild?* My brain failed to understand, he had to spell it in as many words: *Ambika did not appear, Mother. She sent a handmaiden in her place – a woman whose name I never learnt. A woman, more rare and priceless and gracious than any queen; a woman who taught me much across one night, the meaning of words I did not know – words like grace and largesse and parity, some feelings I could never pronounce: desire, shared bliss and harmony; a woman I will not forget easily though I must, I must, to keep my word to the earth and destiny. A woman who will birth a child more than worthy of this dynasty, whom I fear your court and kin will disregard. But that, like other oversights, is their birthright, is it not? I have fulfilled my promise, my last one, and must now withdraw to forget, to forge. It will take me decades of tapas to retrieve my core, become detached and indomitable as sage and bard once more.* Stay one more night, I begged him. Impregnate Ambika again, I begged him. But he smiled in firm denial. *Mother, one thing I learnt yesterday – which I should have as a child (had I been one), or perhaps would, had I grown up by your side – was that no good comes from forcing a woman, even with the noblest of reasons. Ambika does not wish to sleep with me, and it is her heart we should heed.* And with that, he left.

Listen. Listen, rage returned; with it flooded confusion and shame. I was a welter of emotion but before I could recall Ambika to extract an explanation, Poorna appeared at my door: Poorna, Ambika's favourite maid, quiet, astute and full of grace. I had one question. *Were you threatened or offered a bribe?* She replied in usual, unhurried tones: *No, My Queen. It wasn't threat to life, greed, nor lust – as the hazel, restive moon is witness – that thrust me last night through the doors of your son's chamber. It was dread in vile gust, Ambika's dread.* Deferential though she remained, Poorna spoke her mind, her words many-armed, weaponed with truth. Ambika, she revealed, had been driven near mad with alarm at the thought of sex with Vyaasa again – *sanctioned rape,* Poorna termed it – and would have killed herself to avoid any more. Turmoil swirled to guilt in full cascade: the maid did not lie, though I could have burnt her alive for numbering my sins, framing their names and contours, tracing their feet with kumkum. I had transformed from mother to empress; from human to – yes – monarch, ruthless dowager queen obsessed with stock and pedigree, working the lasses under her wing, a son's beloved wives, as – her very words – *fields to be raked, to be furrowed until the perfect fruit was borne.* I had run through the stacked rooms of our past, to pillage other quarters, hurling comets at the futures of unborn sons and sentient daughters. Her words, many-armed, weaponed with truth, still whirl in my mind, jagged edges birthing permanent scabs. I will not expand on that – not all abasement can be shared, however penitent one is. But they stay with me, her words, loyal, deathless sentinels.

Will you have me killed now, or after your grandson's birth? Poorna asked, unruffled as before. I considered her young face with interest, and said, in all honesty, *I do not know yet. We have gone to much too much trouble for a healthy grandchild, it would be a pity to lose him merely to appease my rage and spite your mistress, tempted as I am. Besides, death can be so boring, so swift and uninspiring as punishment. And to make you a martyr would be adverse to crown and kingdom. For now, your pregnancy and childbirth take precedence.* With that, I ended our interview, then marshalled all the king's physicians, the court midwives, to charge them with the handmaid's care. For now, she would have to live and deliver.

Kurukshetra's roots
descend deep; not on earth, but
in Time they belong.

SAUVALI

BEDTIME STORY FOR A DASI'S SON

I.

I have waited long to see you, Child, waited, day after day after day, with little to offer you but this one story, a tale without a distant *once upon a time* to gird it, to keep us safe. *Once* happens, again and again, and will, again. I need you to know how that *once* happens, each moment and each step, so clearly, so intimately, that you become the one within the recursive *once*. They will say you are not old enough to hear these things. But I was not old enough to live them either, and you will not stay young for long, Child. It is better I lead you out of childhood with my own hands, with my words before the world does. And so I wait, Child, I wait to tell you how *once* happened to me, how it happens to my kind. To say

When the king decides to (*say it, say it, say the word,* I tell myself. But I cannot, I find, not yet, at least. I shall begin with periphrases and work my way towards the word. I must begin again.)

II.

When the king decides to take you, the eyes arrive first. Not his own, for he is blind. No, an unkindness of eyes, male and female and other, raptors that circle you, watching, weighing, measuring, probing and prying. An unkindness of eyes, each set different, yet so similar they could all be the same. Eyes that seem to have no tongues, no torsos either though you will feel their beaks inside your head for the rest of your days, pecking your words, gnawing on your thoughts, spitting out syllables, stretching vowels, screeching and cooing in turn, praising and threatening. *It is an honour,* they crow, *that you must strive to deserve. An honour we are so grateful to be spared. A great honour you must not avoid.* You know this already, in all the years you have tried to remain unseen, tried to stay unbodied even when present. For how could you forget your neighbour, the maid who fled, the maid who had reached the river, dived in and nearly crossed its waters when soldiers harpooned her through the neck, hauled her back, then slit her open like a common carp, nose to belly, and left her innards by the bank. For you were taught the tale of your great-aunt, chosen by another monarch many moons back; your great-aunt, who managed to vanish but returned when they fed her husband and her firstborn to a bonfire, feet first – famished bodies flammable as tinder but louder, so much louder – and fed the remains – two tiny hands, a thigh-bone, charred bowels – to red ants. *An honour you cannot refuse,* they caw. As though you don't know that

When the king decides to take
you, there is nowhere to run.
The land is his, the rivers are his[5] – the sky
too, the birds dwelling there bemoan.
When the king decides to take
you, there is nowhere to hide, with earth
and heaven and hell his turf.
When the king decides to take you,
no one comes to the rescue: the gods
are his, myth and legend,
too, his own.

When the king decides to take you, there is much pomp to mark the beginning though not the end. This time, the day and hour must be right, for he must have a child, not just slake his lust. He has waited two years for his pregnant wife to give birth, and he can wait no more. He must have a child, a son, before his brother becomes a father – it is the single goal in his sightless eyes, and so, even a son by a dasi will do. He cannot, this time, grab and ravish you on any given day or night, like nameless, faceless others were ravished in the past: this time, he must be sure his seed is planted right, warn the priests. *You have been chosen*, iterate the eyes in chorus, *from all the virgins in the land – for this time, he will not take the risk of fallow maidens who waste his spore. The priests have named you the most blessed, most fertile of wombs in the kingdom. So you shall bear the king's infant.* Then the eyes grow hands, grow a colony of hands – cold as corpses, swift and sure as cords – to bathe and bedeck, to deck you to be worthy of their king, to perfume your tresses, your wrists, your waist and pastures further south, to rub musk into every inch of skin till you glow with fragrance, with flavour. Anointed, with gold and ghee and sandal. Like a steed for sacrifice, you think, like the prize stallion at an ashwamedha yagna, but for the year of unfettered wandering the equine is first allowed and you are not. But for the pieces of the dead steed offered to the gods, you think, for you cannot be shared: no, all of you must be saved for the king to consume, from navel to nipple to eyelid, insole to clitoris. *And to keep you fecund and faithful, to help you stay focussed and fictile,* the eyes dilate, *your kin – father, brothers, sister-in-law and niece – will be guests of the court, kept in high comfort, though within closed doors.* Just in case you forget

When the king decides to take
you, there is nowhere to run.
The land is his, the rivers are his – the sky
too, the birds dwelling there bemoan.
When the king decides to take
you, there is nowhere to hide, with earth
and heaven and hell his turf.

When the king decides to take you,
no one comes to the rescue: the gods
are his, myth and legend,
too, his own.

When the king decides to (*it is time: say it, say it, say the word,* a voice resounds in my head. Not yet, though. For a word is more than a word, and before it shrapnels my child's ears, he must know its shape and colour, its texture, its smell. So he can hold it, so he can wield it.)

When the king decides to take you, the contours of your life dissolve. You move within a cage of eyes; the unkindness of eyes that define every action, surround you from daybreak to daybreak, from plunder to cleansing to respite to plunder again. Your deflowering, too, is a public act; the bedchamber is not naked nor is the king; only you are. Your deflowering – accompanied by priestly chanting and conch shells – unfolds in three long acts of lunge, grind, rip. The lunge of a Himalayan thing that blots out the night, ferrous hands and knees that unhinge limbs, prying open arms and thighs, no flesh or thought, all metal and sweat and rush. The grind of chest against belly, the grind of seedbags on sepals, the grinding of a back into gravel against silken sheets that singe skin and memory. Rip, the fine robes you were made to wear. Rip, the fragrance of young lips. Rip, softness from both breasts. Rip, the muslin of a heart hidden between two hips, its whorls fluid and dark and furious. Darkness bellows and overflows, till you feel no more. But you wake, all too soon, and when you wake, the king has recommenced, so have the prayers. At first, you know no anger, no fear, only pain that permeates, from skin to marrow. Your spine is bent, bone after bone, with the weight of a tungsten sky. Your breasts have aged, the nipples turned to rust. Mouth and tongue swell into rubble and dust. Your back and neck bear the hieroglyphics of talons: deep and live and rubescent, the kingdom's untold history. Your belly is a molten, screaming pit that cannot be hushed.

When the king decides to rape you, no one will use the word *rape*. The word does not exist in the king's world. Your body is just another province he owns, from navel to nipple to eyelid, insole to clitoris. And it is not over yet. Time moves from night to night, from one coupling to the next. For you are to be pounded till you procreate. Each night, he comes to peel then split you open like a tangerine, suck dry then discard all thought of you except the seed. Each night, you must try to be pliant – for a king's displeased voice can sever heads. Each night, you curse the queen whose unending incubation has forced you to her husband's bed. Each night, you pity the queen whose husband knows no tenderness, no love in his loins save for a son and heir. Each night. Till the day the priests announce you are child-bound, and the delicate state removes you from the king's chambers. For nine months, you are precious, the bight of your belly the altar at which the eyes, the unkindness of eyes, dance and bow. Then, one day, you are not. Your son has dehisced: a slash of earth – red, ripe and viscous – that swims out from the sea above your legs. And the queen's hundred sons burst forth from their capsules. The dearth of infants is over. Court and kingdom rejoice. Court and kingdom expel you and your kin to the outer boundaries of the land, with a fistful of gold to keep you well away from your son. But you return. You return, again and again, until the queen, who fears your being, promises the child can visit you, so you will not cast a shadow on her realm. So you wait, you wait for the day he will make that journey to your hut, to your heart. Each day, you wait, with tireless gaze scorching the path to your hut. Each day, you clean the bare insides of your home till they gleam in pain. Each day, you repeat the story you will tell your son, even as you hear the distant chant of the unkindness of eyes.

When the king decides to take
you, there is nowhere to run.
The land is his, the rivers are his – the sky
too, the birds dwelling there bemoan.

When the king decides to take
you, there is nowhere to hide, with earth
and heaven and hell his turf.
When the king decides to take you,
no one comes to the rescue: the gods
are his, myth and legend,
too, his own.

III.

When the king decides to rape me or my kind, no one will use the word *rape*. The word does not exist in the king's world. This body is just another province he owns, from navel to nipple to eyelid, insole to clitoris.

But even the king cannot own a thought, nor a conscience – nobody can. This, I tell myself, night and day, Child, even today. It is the amulet that kept me sane through my time in the palace; it is the amulet I will tie on your wrist when you arrive, my real bequest. When the time comes, Child, you can unwrite the end of this tale, unravel the letters, invent a new script. For truth can crawl out of slush, shed gravity and soar. And, for one night, remember, ants too can take wing – that is a choice you will have as well.

GANDHARI

THE DEADLINESS OF BROKEN THINGS

If only they'd killed you when you were still a child,
my brother, my almost-son. There are times I think
I have been walking with your grave these many years.
Were you not the only being to know my name,

Shakuni, my brother, I think all my sons could
still live long and prosper, though Kuru would then bloom.
But you'd known my being, my name, my true name: not
Gandhari, the dead suffix to land I've become.

So I prayed you'd live long, prosper – and doom Kurus
who'd slain and drawn Father, our brothers, then quartered
Gandhar to dead, annexed land. You've become that day
of ruin: you came undone – the sun torn from its seams,

when our kin, our earth and skies were drawn and quartered
at Bheeshma's hands. They owned our eyes: the shattered skulls,
the torn lungs, arms ruined and legs undone, the sons crushed
in live wombs; and eyes, eyes all over, unfurled, gouged,

handless, shattered; eyes that clamoured for Bheeshma's skull
in single, splattered tongue and never left our heads.
Eyes haunted my womb and unfurled our hearts to gouge
lost names – what else could they do? We're their last refuge.

By Father's splattered head, in gashed tongue, I swore not
to glimpse the world again. Eyes I bound in revenge –
blindness was my last refuge. What could Bheeshma do,
save praise his blind nephew's captive bride and name my

bound, vengeful eyes love's crown? Eyes the world glimpsed again
no more: none had seen the sun in my twilight gaze
save you, captive kin of blind Dhritarashtra's bride –
a wounded, brooding child who would scarce walk or speak.

You were the sun at midnight: my last gaze, no more
sights would breach the silk band on my eyes, nor my heart
that spoke only to this child whose wounds walked barefoot
to hell, loath to heal. While I, I was filled with night:

lone sight to breach silk-banded eyes. Night sang in heart
and vein, night played bass at my forced wedding, my wake.
I'd dance with my loathed spouse to hell, unhealing night
by our side: this I swore. No love, no ruth flowed through

my veins for the prince I was forced to wed, whose wake
had engulfed my name, my kin, my land – my whole world.
Ruthless though my oath, *the flow of selfless love* swore
and sang the bards: I became the wife who'd renounced

sight, kin, land – her whole world – to gulf the unnamed tides
that trapped her man, to share his tragic lot. Kingdom
and clan sang with the bards: renouncer wives became
high fashion – with other Kuru brides made to match

my tragic lot. King Pandu's two queens had to share
exile from crown and coupling, then gift themselves to
others – Kuru-fashion – so their bridegroom could match
his forefathers in fruit. If I could, I'd have picked

exile from coition, a real gift when crowned
my husband's spouse: thrust, grind, rip – brutal, the nightly
forays in his thirst for fruit, his need to father
kings, to beat his kid brother to that coveted

spot. My spouse whose brutal nights ripped more maidenheads
while my belly rounded with his seed's lifetime – slow
beating, such birthing of kings. Covetous, Brother,
and quiet were your hands, as they settled their eyes

on my round belly, slowed with Dhritarashtra's seed.
Then came the infants, all hundred and one, restored
by Vyaasa's quiet hands; settled, all, with hale eyes –
softly, I thanked gods I had disowned for a while.

All hundred and one, my infants, come to restore –
bit by unsought bit – hope, warmth, care: stars for my night,
soft gifts from gods I tried not to own, at first, while
battling madly for their lives, mainly the eldest's.

The stars presaged he'd benight the earth: drain hope, warmth
and goodness from our land. A demon reborn who'd
battle all his life; our eldest, mad with greed, would
tear the age apart, so Vidur and Vyaasa said.

*Demons, once born, must be slain, for the good of land
and race*, they urged. *Kill the child*, they urged. *Kill him now,
save our age*, so Vidur and Vyaasa said. Untorn,
for once, my husband and I were firm in response:

*This child won't be killed. Not for race, nor earth. Now urge
no further. Cherish Suyodhan as our crown prince.*
Just once more would I hear my husband respond – firm,
regal – thus. By then, he'd be moving to the swirl

of your words – prized, by crown and prince (even further
under your spell) heedless of other counsel, both
right and regal. Every word, thus, a designed move,
the arabesque of a sword seeking to avenge

through heedful counsel all our other kin, to spell
an end to Kuru. At ten – broken-hearted, maimed,
you'd sought to slay their sun, and venge the arabesques
of voices stilled in Gandhar. While I, who'd tried gloom

and noon to drown my maimed heart and break the Kuru
reign, now find it flaming blue-black by dusk again,
stoked by gladness, stilled since Gandhar. But I'd tried in
vain. Love kindles constellations on my moonless

vault; its reign flames, blue-gold through dusk and newfound dawn.
It didn't happen overnight, Brother. After
vain, long moons could my sons kindle and constellate
fresh memories for me, atolls of the present.

But you, Brother, night after night, you happen – steeped
in hate. Revenge is the sole land you'll populate.
Your present – future memories tolling defeat
and serfage – to Suyodhan feeds him distrust, greed

and hate, revenge for land he cannot populate.
I've begged you to desist: not to make murderers
of my sons; Suyodhan serf to distrust and greed.
Why destroy them when Bheeshma and Dhritarashtra

are our foes, I begged. *Desist from the cold murder
of innocents, whether Pandav or Kaurav*, I
begged. *Grief alone destroys Bheeshma, Dhritarashtra
and their kind*, you replied, unforgiving as Time.

There are no innocents, Pandav or Kaurav, you
replied, *in this world save the unborn. Only fools
forgive, for men are crueller than Time. Kindness
is wasted on Kuru, where fathers leach sons' lives,*

you replied, *in a world where fools are born as kings.*
All of you gleams murder: your eyes are spears; your mouth,
a dagger. The perfect son, you'll waste Kuru lives –
your words a silver sabre. You are a death Death

would die to kiss: murderous mouth and gleaming eyes,
skin glinting vitreous. There is no stopping you,
your words spell slow death, death from a broken sabre.
Death propelled, impartially, at your sons and mine –

you'll not stop with others' kin, vitreous the glint
of wrath and loathing that keeps you breathing. But how
can the Kuru stay impartial to death propelled,
unmindful of your lethal, silk tongue? Suyodhan,

clothed in loathing, breathes only wrath; Dhritarashtra
drowns in woe – they deem all your doomsday ploys the truth.
No one disarms your lethal mind, your silken web
of lies, not Bheeshma, not the court. Even Krishna

never deploys the truth to drown your doomsday plots.
I asked Kunti, once, to step in, to save her sons
from lies, to goad Bheeshma and the court or Krishna
to see sense: she preferred Kuru sectioned, with her

sons lords of a wasteland, than to step back here, save
as kings, she said. They'd barely survived death by fire:
this time, she preferred safety to sense, to section
their life well away from Hastina. That was when

I knew we'd not survive. Kingship – not dearth, not fire –
and you would be our nemesis. The king pronounced
a life away from Hastina – Indraprastha,
new kingdom on barren land – for the five Pandav:

the pronouncement of nemesis, the king does not
see, but then he never did. For I know, distance
from the Pandav will not turn barren the kingdom
of my son's greed. And you'll not rest till haemic light –

more distant from insight and joy there'll never be –
rains, till it shatters earth into a million eyes,
till unrest and greed spill haemic light from our sons.
If I could, I'd halt Time, force him back to the day

a million eyes rained on Gandhar's earth to carve out
your grave that I have been carrying for all these years,
made heavier each day. I'd force Time to halt, return,
and I'd kill you myself while you were still a child.

SATYAVATI

X . FAULT LINES

Eighteen years. Eighteen more years of joy and colour I own in my heart. Eighteen years when my blood smiled and flourished. Years of peace and pride and prosperity as Hastina healed, little by little, from the grief and fear and febrility of quick royal deaths and ownerless crowns. Joy, but the quiet, grateful joy of those who dare not exult too much, having met all too often the baneful underside of bliss. We would not, I think, ever again believe – or not fully, at least – in the benevolence of Fate and our numberless deities, so we savoured, bit by delectable bit (each as though it were the last), the flavour of every day without a tragedy. I watched Vidura, Pandu and Dhritarashtra – my grandsons, born to Poorna, Ambalika and Ambika – grow; grow, each in his own way, into leviathans. Each so different, but his brothers' missing segment – together they were an infrangible inconel bolt. I watched Bheeshma step into painfully familiar – though fond – shoes, those of preceptor, of near-parent. This time, though, he really did keep his heart in quarantine: he lavished learning and skills, wisdom and statecraft on his nephews, but withheld the warmth and tenderness, for most part, except to the throne. I watched Ambika and Ambalika recover, timorous and disbelieving at first, from the couplings I'd enjoined of them; recover and ripen into dowagers, sure and stately. And Poorna, whose life I had spared – unreasonably, rued the court at first – despite the deception; I watched her bequeath an age-old, quiet serenity on her son. I watched and rejoiced, and wondered how long it could all last, and rejoiced all the same.

Listen. Listen, then came the time to coronate the next suzerain, when Bheeshma and I crossed words once again, for Bheeshma stood obdurate that Pandu should be made king, and I insisted otherwise, convinced of a reign by triumvirate. Only an able-bodied, blue-blooded prince should be crowned monarch, persisted Bheeshma, and Dhritarashtra, though impeccable of breeding and strong of reasoning, was born blind, and the sightless could not rule, declared our regent. While Vidura, ablest, most astute and heaven-sent of the three siblings, bore not a trace of kshatriya blood in his being – his mother was a dasi, Bheeshma bemoaned, and the father, whilst a legendary sage, had fisher-stock in his veins. And wasn't Pandu, I retorted, though invincible a warrior, too reckless to be king – not to mention, as we alone knew, unfit to produce heirs? Let them, I urged, rule together – each redeeming the others' failings. Besides, I cautioned, to be removed from crown and throne would gnarl Dhritarashtra's soul, maim him more than blindness ever could and lead him to loathe his kin. That, Bheeshma countered, was no reason he should be named sovereign – kingship was not an exercise in self-affirmation, it was the kingdom he had to consider. The kingdom, came my response, would not survive a heart that spurned its own blood. Our words snarled. Our words glared. Our words circled, baying for full victory. There they stood – bare-clawed, fanged, tentacled, eager to pounce and rent when, all of a sudden, I tired.

Listen, I tired of the whole rigmarole, of the mausoleum of a future that pressed on my pharynx. I tired of my actions, tired of our lynxlike words, tired of watching my choices tumble in the wind, a stalk of ants clinging to the tune of a dented lute. I would not, I said to myself, stand in the way of Bheeshma's convictions, nor press my case further – it was his turn to take the reins of choice for kin and country, to feel free to unleash errors and revel in his own decisions. It was a strange floweret, this fatigue that had so rapidly bloomed without discernible root or calyx: a fatigue that threatened to overwhelm my words, my purpose. I had to retreat, I saw, with the daybreak of clarity, retreat to quieter times, at least for a while. But I couldn't, not just yet, for there was a slew of ceremonies, and my absence, Bheeshma averred, would be read as dissent by court and kingdom – with the queen-mother's discord a heady stimulant for future disaffection, he held. Order, he insisted, must be maintained whatever the cost to personal feelings or well-being. So I stayed, and saw, and saw differently, through eyes cleansed by tiredness and distance. Words eluded me, but not thought. I saw rage and shame shimmer in Dhritarashtra's chest, nerves channelling dark fuel from heart to limbs each day. I saw Pandu's inborn pride sediment into hubris. I saw the court dance obeisance to the king, quietly disregarding the eldest prince, more and more each day. I saw them scoff at the youngest, the lowborn one, I saw them revile him more brazenly each day, and there I intervened once again: I bid Bheeshma designate Vidura prime minister of Kuru, central pillar of Hastina's court – an office independent of birth. He agreed, instantly, as I'd hoped he would: if it didn't menace his cherished social stasis, Bheeshma was happy to espouse efficiency, even a simulacrum of equality.

Then, I left. I left with Poorna and an entourage of soldiers, charioteers, cooks, physicians and loyal servants. I left, but not before exhorting Bheeshma to pay twice-fold heed to Dhritarashtra's hopes and dreams – the boy's wounds could still heal, deep and putrid though they throbbed. *Do what it takes*, I pressed, *to make him happy again, if you want to keep this kingdom whole. Dhritarashtra is a man of mighty but slow passions: while he will not detonate overnight his hate can corrode the bedrock of this dynasty. Do not let him get steeped in self-pity – that will spell collective doom. There is unbridled love in his heart, but make no mistake; the venin that looms in his blood is just as potent. Do not give it room to rise to his troubled mind. Do not let him find his way to sin.* And with that, I left, voyaging first to the sacred sites where the ancient rivers meet: it was time, I felt, to thank all the forces that had kept hope alive, and perhaps pray – pray, like I never had, to an ambush of gods I still did not entirely trust – for that cascade of blessings to keep flowing. Thence, to Prayaga we travelled, confluence of Ganga, Yamuna and Saraswathi, said the sages, consecrated by nectar from the gods during the cosmic churning; Prayaga, whose waters could wash all vice and sin, they swore.

(Though people there, I found – unsurprised, on the whole – were not specially devout, not more, that is, than in any other spot; all the sacred waters had little effect on the thieves and louts who scavenged around its hallowed banks. Salvation, I thought once again, was unlike a king; it would not tread on unwelcoming ground, much less pitch its pennant.) From Prayaga, we moved to Kashi, childhood city of Ambika and Ambalika, then from there, further southwest, to Somnath and the warm climes of Kamboj.

Listen. Listen, several years passed, years of quiet and peace and discovery. It was – let's not pretend – invigorating to shed the mantle of the land I'd worn for more years than I could count, to wander the realm unattended by royal cares, to have to withstand merely cyclones and fierce mountains, marauding bands and the odd, rampaging bull-elephant. And the company of rivers, after such a long hiatus, appeased both heart and mind – it was little short of a family reunion, I'd never felt so much at ease since the early demise of my younger sons. But our halcyon existence was to cease, for all too soon, came Bheeshma's urgent summons – the duta Ajay, his private messenger (reliable, if young), caught up with us on the route to Madurai. Ajay had never been one to equivocate or stand on protocol. *Queen Mother,* he submitted, *Lord Bheeshma begs you to return forthwith. Maharani Gandhari has been pregnant for two years, and shows no signs yet of parturition. King Dhritarashtra's frenzy to attain fatherhood before his brother knows no bounds; he had soldiers and priests scour the land for the most fertile maiden to beget his children since the Maharani has been, begging your pardon, somewhat inadequate. Lord Bheeshma feels you are the only person who can prevent him from further folly.* It sounded like a clutter of conundrums to me, all mewling for attention. Maharani Gandhari? A two-year pregnancy? King Dhritarashtra? *King?* How did that transpire when Bheeshma was so unyielding on the issue of blind monarchs? And where was Pandu? When did he stop being king? My questions tumbled faster than Ganga's rapids up north. It was Ajay's turn to look baffled. Hadn't we met with the many messengers Lord Bheeshma had unfailingly sent through the years to announce each event, joyful or tragic? None ever returned to Hastina, but all our carrier pigeons had reached home, so no one felt any dread, though Bheeshma wondered now and then why I hadn't sent my blessings to all the newlyweds.

Listen, the boy lost no time filling us in on the last seven years of Hastina's annals. Dhritarashtra, soon after we had left, expressed a tender regard for the Princess of Gandhar, a maiden – sang the bards – so virtuous and dazzling that Lord Shiva himself had appeared to grant her a boon: not two or a dozen, but a hundred sons would she bear, he'd promised. Dhritarashtra had merely heard of her charms, but Bheeshma gathered, that'd been enough for heart and mind to disarm. Steadfast to my adjurations on saving the blind prince from fatal gloom, Bheeshma sent the King of Gandhar a generous bid for his daughter's hand – so certain of the impending nuptials (Kuru much mightier than a far-off mountain land), he even had a palace built for the future couple. Therein perhaps the wrath – crimson, cataclysmic – that reared unbidden when he received Gandhar's rebuff, clear as the streams in that high country: *No daughter of mine will be made to wed a blind man, at least not during my lifetime, however vast the wingspan of his kingdom or treasury.*

It was a carnage, said Ajay, as ever deadpan. *They never stood a chance.* For out marched Bheeshma, Pandu at his flanks, both in deathly martial trance, with the entire Kuru army, falling on the Gandhar citadel with more hunger and savagery than a shiver of tiger sharks. Adults and children and the ancient were decimated – even-handed were my kinsmen in bloodlust – beginning with the father who'd stated *not in my lifetime,* who met an end both slow and barbarous. The epoch they slaughtered drowned Gandhar's mountains in claret. The Kuru forces returned victorious with Princess Gandhari, and her sole living kin: her youngest brother, a lame, solemn child named Shakuni. *Why did Bheeshma spare his life,* I asked, curious at such largesse when so many waifs had been slain. *It was his sister's only address when we reached the palace,* recalled Ajay, *she begged he be spared, she begged to see his face before she embraced sightlessness to match each step with her future husband. You see, she chose to wear a blindfold for the rest of her life. Lord Bheeshma was deeply stirred by her spousal devotion, he was ready to grant her every wish – but he'd already razed her kin and kingdom, so there wasn't much else of a request.* A shiver ran through my breasts on hearing his description: what kind of human blinds herself from fealty to a man she'd never met, a man she'd been forced to wed over the shattered lives and severed heads of her clan?

The duta's next account impinged on my ruminations. *Lord Bheeshma then sought brides for King Pandu and Prime Minister Vidura.* Vidura, though, found a wife all on his own – the younger sister of a ground landlord from another province, a damsel sound in scriptures, gentle, gracious. A union renowned in Hastina, their well deserved bliss soon crowned by two infants. Pandu, I learnt, followed his uncle's bidding to the last syllable. First sent by Bheeshma to King Kuntibhoja's court, he vied for – and won – the winsome, doe-eyed Princess Kunti's heart and lot. A year later, Ajay added, Bheeshma married Pandu off once more: for a king, he thought, needed more than one consort (both as strategic alliance and after-life insurance). The second bride, for some reason, had to be bought, and Princess Madri – fragrant and voluptuous as Usha, the dawn goddess – got from the Kuru coffers several chests of gold and pearl and coral, wrought-iron arms and a war elephant. Everyone in Madra and Kuru – save Kunti, whose opinions were not sought – called it a match made in heaven. Before he could fully savour his uxorious haven, Pandu, alas, had to lead a conquest of another kind; turn invader on kingdoms near and far at Bheeshma's behest. Kashi (yes, once again: that land could find no rest), Anga, Vanga and Kalinga, Magadha and Dasarna (which had shown no signs of unrest): the Kuru escutcheon quelled regions all over Bharatavarsha.

You'd think he'd weary after so much mayhem, but Pandu was, it appeared, a true Kuru – in spirit, if not by blood. After the nationwide rampage, he left with both his brides on an extended hunt in the northern mountains, his notion of the perfect honeymoon. It was the silly season for venery. Pandu would kill by day and conjugate by moonlight – a pleasing arrangement for everyone, from wives to cooks to servitors. One morning, let's say, a rare, soft morning in beryl, claret and cream, with the gods alas, once again! – at play in some other clime, Pandu – like many a royal ancestor – went off to hunt, as kings are wont. He chased and stalked, trapped, shot and killed. Having killed and killed again, littered the land with dead hart and doe, tiger, partridge, even crow, he spotted a sudden movement in the clearing. Sighting a stag and hind rutting, musk deer, he thought, as the male mounted his eager, quivering mate. Slighting the first, sacred law of the hunt, *never seek or attack animals in the throes of passion*, the king – drunk on an altogether deadlier potion – sent an arrow through both their loving groins.

Listen. Listen, even Pandu, practised killer that he was, felt his flesh congeal as a bestial scream tore the earth apart. Stag and hind, mangled and bleeding, transformed into man and woman kneeling and shuddering – and still bleeding – before Pandu's startled eyes: it was a rishi and his wife, who'd turned into deer to prolong the pleasure of coition, their favoured sport and pastime, a lethal one, alas, in these godless climes. Alas, alas, for them, there was just an agonising, unsatiated end ahead – but the rishi struck back with the last remnants of his breath. *Cruel, heartless king, you who know it is forbidden to hunt animals in rut, a sin to attack couples that are mating, may you die the instant you try copulating with your wife or concubine. May you learn to pine for your beloved's touch, may you yearn to spill your seed into a woman. May you drown each night in torment for this malign deed.* And with that vicious curse, the rishi perished on his dead lover's breasts. Alas, alas for Pandu, he could neither repent nor repine. It was the end of his dreams of greater glory, and very nearly the end of his story. The king abjured his crown, he sent back his royal guards and priests, attendants and ministers, he would have sent his wives too if he could, but Kunti and Madri clung on to him as vines do to a peepul, vowing that celibacy by his side would be their chosen lot. They renounced all earthly possessions, removed weapons and silks and gold from their persons, and swore to live as sanyasis, swore to become hermits without human desires.

That, Ajay continued, *is how Prince Dhritarashtra was crowned king of Kuru, overlord of much of Bharatavarsha, of all the kingdoms his brother had won in his last, triumphal march.* And yet, and yet, although he dwelled in the heart of the Himalayas with a mortal curse over his head, it was Pandu who, unwittingly (or perhaps not, could it really be that innocent?) had designed

the current frenzy in Dhritarashtra's mind. Two
years and a bit earlier, the news had arrived that
Kunti was pregnant – wandering ascetics had
brought the good news. Bheeshma hailed it as
divine intervention, and rewarded the messengers
lavishly but Dhritarashtra, oddly, tried to slay
them with bare arms. Strange things began to
happen: Gandhari, also pregnant, would camber
and grow and stretch, a near full moon, but her
babies remained unborn – this after the twenty-
first month, while Dhritarashtra had grown
malignant with despair and envy. And when the
king heard – this time through spies – that Kunti
would soon deliver her firstborn, Pandu's son, he
frothed like one possessed. The queen had then
sworn she'd tear her belly rather than see him bed
another woman, when she'd heard of the new –
priestly-sanctioned – scheme for an heir. That was
when Bheeshma, in desperation, had deemed it
time to summon me back.

Listen, I heard the full account, and I saw a vortex,
a wave, a leap tide of metal; a ripple of stones and
pebbles in spume. Rock warriors would rise, I
could hear their chant in my bones, many-armed
and lethal, they would fling meteors at brothers
and lovers, fathers and grandsons. I could see the
sun melt into the sea, and a giant orb of slag engulf
his seat on the horizon. I could see the earth go
blind. In that instant, the future sang to me in a
voice of flint, sharp and thin and sulphurous. I
could see all of it – every wound and want and
villainy that lurked ahead. It was pralaya that
gestated in Kunti's and Gandhari's wombs, not
children, not heirs. This was a gift I had never

desired, that even I – with all my failings – did not deserve, the gift of such clear prophecy as dreamt of by seers. Why could the gods – if they really did exist – not choose another being? Now I would have to return even as I could hear my body crumble, its words dissolve and tremble, the letters unreel, the curlicues trail and fade into nothing. There was little I could do, but I had to return. I had to return. *We ride at dawn, I declared, we ride at dawn despite flash floods and the approaching monsoon. There are greater dangers than inclement weather ahead. Send word to Bheeshma.*

Brothers will duel
in dharma's name – low, the cost
of moral victory.

HIDIMBI

RESIDUUM (EPISTLES)

(i)

For it is spring,
   Kirmira. For it is
      spring in Hidimbavana

again. Not the first
   spring, for Chaitra has been
      before, many a time – and will

leave again. But for now,
   the roots smell moist and green,
      while earth blossoms, ripe and eager

underfoot. The rivers return,
   younger, tamer, with a sky tender
      to the touch. Alongside jasmine and rose

and magnolia, hope spreads
   in seven shades. Birdsong lights
      the ears, no more cold, silent dread.

For Hidimba is dead. Relief
   washes me like rain. Brother he was, but
      only in name. I lived in fear for my being,

that you know well, not unlike
   the wild boar and gazelle, nishadas,
      rakshasas, even gandharvas who throng

these woods. If famished, he would
   have supped on his sister's flesh, and swigged
      this blood. Life had become a constant hunt – I spent

my hours like a hound, chasing
   and killing, skinning beasts to slake
      such an endless thirst, could only scramble

after pelt and bone, suck
   their remains once he was done.
      It would end, I had always thought,

some day soon, but not
   this way: I hadn't hoped to survive
      my monstrous sibling.

For one day, they appeared,
   Kirmira, six majestic orchids amongst
      ruderals: a woman with five men, bipeds

in the guise of gods or kinnaras.
   We caught sandal and musk, rose,
      heliotrope in the air from their hide.

Hidimba rose and sank
   with new appetite, bid me
      to seize the whole unseen lot,

to prepare this unseasonal
   feast of human flesh. I had killed
      men before, though I didn't care

too much for their brawn – too
   pallid, too fat, too cloyingly sweet.
      But who'd defy Hidimba and risk

their tongue? Off I loped
    to gather the prey from a nearby
        copse, five recumbent figures at the feet

of a – oh! My sweet breath, I saw –
    a demigod. I drank in the landscape
        of his shoulders, his arms, his neck,

the acreage in his chest, the peak
    between his legs and I was struck –
        struck instantly, insatiably by lust; struck

hard enough
    to make me want
        to save their lives.

For you know, Kirmira, I can
    morph into earth, into insect, into ocean,
        crone, enchantress. I could have transformed

into a goddess to entice him – but
    I didn't need to (Never mind the lore
        as often, it lies). Instead, I begged to carry him far

away, away from Hidimba's fangs
    and belly. I begged to hide him in the wind,
        amidst rivulets, begged this man – Bheema,

Son of Pandu, once a prince
    of the Kuru lands, he introduced himself –
        to flee but he would not wake his sleeping family,

their rest he priced more
   than a kingdom, he said. And at that,
      Hidimba arrived, a tempest of teeth and claws

and fury, aiming to slice me
   for having tarried with the quarry.
      He didn't understand, my brother for whom all

life was meat (a future meal,
   at worst), how desire could swallow
      fear, snap that slender tendon of consanguinity.

But he never reached
   my skin – Bheema stepped
      into his path, toppled him as earthquakes

upend mountains. They grappled
   and girned, loud enough to rouse volcanoes,
      dry up oceans – loud enough to wake the Pandu

sons, who leapt up with supernal
   arms. But, it was over before they could
      dilute the duel – Bheema picked Hidimba

by the hind, and rent him
   from head to penis, like a
      voiceless, powerless stalk.

For Bheema did not fight
   to save me: I would not have
      loved him if he had. He battled –

as always – to protect his clan.
   The rest, Kirmira, was swift – I
      cannot lie, I did not regret my brother's

demise, nobody in this forest
   did. I declared my love, in words
      clear and steady. Bheema declined

my hand at first, though his eyes
   signalled ample interest. He called me
      rakshasi, demon-sorceress. Their mother

intervened, *Phir bhi yeh naari hai*,[6]
   she reminded: nonetheless, she is – and
      above all – a woman. We were wedded

with her blessings that very day.

I knew this night had to leave one day.
A tawny moon would walk off with you
and yours, Bheema, as my blood flowed grey:
I knew this. Night has to leave one day
for battle – and you must lead the way,
you, the clan's dagger, their flame, this too
I know. But don't leave tonight. One day,
soon, the new moon can walk off with you.

(iii)

I returned him, Kirmira,
    returned him to the Pandavas,
        a year and four months later, returned all

of Bheema, or almost. His broad,
    straight back, eloquent only in lust. Eyes
        unfurrowed, sprightly with daybreak. The smile

that lights him, down to
    the fingertips. Both legs, planted wide –
        sturdy as the unseen roots of mountains – or

right-angled for chase.
    Arms unquiet, even when at rest.
        Branches of ribs that would blossom

around my breasts. The doubt,
    the sorrow, the lurking unworth
        of second-born, never best, thrumming

in his blood. Then his lungs,
    which had soared on love's fragrance.
        A full-throated delight in the shimmer,

the heights of my unvanquished
    world – her endless oceans, her orotund
        wilds, the earthly summits and celestial designs,

trees that deliquesce in moonlight:
    the sounds, the smells, the sights I unveiled
        dawn, noon and early dark for four months and

a year (his family, strange, irrational
    beings, never let him stay full nights
        with me – they feared a rakshasi's power

would turn him into plaything
   if he spent all four prahars by her side).
      All I kept are shorn filaments from both

hearts, intertwined and grown
   into trust. And a son, who, anyway,
      would be mine. Bheema's family had no use

for children until they turned
   harvestable: biddable, weddable,
      or expendable, machines of war.

I gave him hunt and forage
   as parting gifts, Kirmira: never would
      Bheema hunger in the wilds again, nor his clan.

I taught him smell. The odour
   of roe and rabbit, of morel and toadstool,
      the distant hint of petrichor. Scents of chestnut,

of resin, of wild elephant
   in rut. Venom in half-bloom on
      nervous, beckoning petals. The nidor

in enemy sweat, the mute
   smell of death. Taught him
      touch. Taught him to read tales

of a royal courtship from lion's
   spoor, to relive the songs of centuries
      with fingers on the whorls of a murdered

tree. Taught him speed, then
   accuracy. And mercy, to kill
      rapidly, without leisure or display.

Kill, for need and not
   for pleasure. Enough
      and never any more.

We rakshasas labelled
   bloodthirsty, savage, take fewer
      lives than royals, I proved, time after

time. (Except the odd
   fiend like Hidimba, who gave
      our race a bad name.) And Bheema

learnt, learnt quick and well.
   Like a child unpraised all his days,
      he basked in my urging, my applause.

I never called him
   dense, nor thick-headed,
      never dismissed his thoughts –

tried, silently, to erode
   a lifetime of blithe hurt his brothers
      had gifted, the reward humans so easily

inflict on slower kin. Confidence
   my final offering, a lasting dowry.
      So then they left. Left in pursuit

of justice, life and the greater
   glory they believed was theirs
      from birth. The woman and five men,

all hers to command.
   Yuddhishtira, the righteous,
      their future king, who'd quoted

scriptures to endorse my rights
   to Bheema when he'd seemed
      unwilling to wed (demurral, I learnt

later, my husband's tested
   ploy to secure elder approval).
      Bheema, next, cannier by far than

his brothers inferred, but gentle,
   wistful, and more loyal than anyone
      deserved. The balletic Arjuna, sharp yet

unsure (for all that self-love)
   beneath his archer's aegis – a man
      in need of a word, or a god, though

he knew it not. With Nakula
   and Sahadeva, dissimilar twins,
      still callow, still unfinished, blurred

composites of the older siblings.
   All satellites, Kirmira, orbiting
      their mother Kunti, the heliacal force.

I watched them leave, relief –
    I must admit – in king tide
        submerging both love's ache

and vinculum. I have a forest
    to rule, Kirmira, with land more
        vast, more populous than Hastina –

though scarce visible
    to my in-laws' eyes, now
        urbanite – and a child to raise

as earthling, as chieftain.
    And the Pandavas, I had come
        to see, required too often too much.

Besides they could help
    with neither task: these men
        were to remain sons, at best brothers –

they could seldom grow
    into husbands, and never
        fathers. Their own kingship,

I can foretell, will be steered
    by possession, loss and carnage,
        death tolls the pennant for success.

No, it was best to bid them adieu,
    though it isn't quite that – some ties
        stay unsevered, even when tattered.

(iv)

I am writing to you from tomorrow,
Queen, Mother, land of stippled delights where
summer dances in my son's eyes, they glow

farther than the Karthigai.[7] The echo
of that light swathes earth, scours the solitaire
I am. Writing to you from tomorrow,

I fret: can we keep him from the shadow
his fathers will throw? Find Forever's lair
before summer's dance ends? My son's eyes glow

just like yours, while his laughter – full and slow –
is all Bheem. Of this first grandchild, your heir,
I'll keep writing to you. From tomorrow

he'll learn to transform: become fire, arrow,
dragon – swift and dire; for vast power, snare
summer, and dance in the sun's eyes – their glow

will fill his veins. Whom the gods thus bestow,
they also erase – it's this torment's glare
I am writing to you from. Tomorrow,
though, summer dances: my son's eyes will glow.

Summer has left
   our eyes, Kirmira.
      Autumn bestrides

the earth, bestrides my skin,
   blazing miles of chinar and memories.
      Blood – or vermilion, I cannot say which –

smudges night, its clutter
   of stars, and a sightless,
      stumbling moon. Death has

returned, further south,
   with a maiden and five
      weddings: it is Kunti

who tells me so. We write,
   yes, the queen-mother and I,
      we write and share, trading imprints

the other will not see –
   she of her son, often sons;
      I of mine. Of kingship, conquests

and queens. The history of
   the hunt. Stories of hunter and
      hunted no poet-sages nor scribes

seem to sing. I am sorry,
   Kirmira, yes, you heard right:
      Bakasura was slain, in the jungles

of Ekachakra. His belly slathered
   on the forest floor, limbs sliced and
      diced and doused in gore, eyes plucked

out, head skewered
   on a branch of sal. My spies
      sent home that very headline. Yet

another rakshasa king,
   you mourn. Yes, one more
      rakshasa, and one more brother,

estranged though you both
   remained. Brother and ruler
      but cannibal and cruel, he had – you

agree – dived headfirst to hell,
   and dragged his world with him,
      lower still: a wilder, fouler despot

than Hidimba himself, feasting
   on his own people week after week,
      for years. Bheema slew him, the excrescence.

I do not blame him, not for that
   act of expunction. There is no real
      solution for the Baka of this earth.

But the relish in the kill;
   the gleeful, long dismembering;
      this defiling of spent flesh – that spells

a new Bheem, one who kills
   not like warrior nor beast but man,
      one I had never quite seen.

It was hunger, insisted
    Kunti. The hunger that walked
        with the brahmin guise they had

to don in the hamlet,
    Ekachakra, feeding off alms
        from kindly strangers, or poor

neighbours. Yes, I thought,
    hunger, or the fury that kept
        spiralling in his gut, eyes unblinking,

tongue manacled. The villagers did
    not feel my fear: they jubilated, fêting
        Bheem's victory, the revelry spreading far

and deep, alongside tales of a nameless,
    matchless brahmin lad, saviour of the suffering
        masses, till the Pandavas – dreading fame, discovery –

fled silently one night, south
    to Kampilya, heart of Panchala,
        straight into the arms of their dazzling,

deadly future: twin pairs
    of arms. First, a consort, Draupadi,
        dredged from the bowels of earth and fire

by a vengeful parent,
    by artful deities. Draupadi,
        goddess of tenebrous flame,

the reward Arjuna received
  from Drupada, Panchala's king,
    for striking the eye of a spinning,

wooden carp, strung high up
  above the heads of royal suitors
    gathered to win her jewelled hand.

(Yes, Kirmira, that's how humans
  pick husbands for their daughters and
    name it *swayamvara*, the bride's own choice.)

Draupadi, thus gained by Arjuna,
  both saved by Bheema from hordes
    of petulant rulers and princes. Draupadi,

then divided between five
  brothers as bride, to heed Kunti's
    behest, *Share and share alike, all alms,*

all earnings, today as always.
  Draupadi, who will have
    to offer, then, heart and hymen,

over and over, to five
  men she never chose (nor,
    really, did the lifeless fish that

defined her lot), all
  for a mother's word to stay
    true. When questioned, Kunti

wrote to me, *One queen*
   to bind them all: that, my sons
     will always need, and it must now

be one other than me.
   And with Draupadi
     comes Krishna as dowry:

Krishna, their secret arm,
   king-maker, counsellor, chief Yadava,
     lord of the cow-herder tribes, controller –

I begin to hear – of the land's
   destiny. Stay well away, Kirmira, from
     Krishna's gaze. The Yadava bodes well

for neither forests
   nor forest-dwellers like us.
     He lobs winter with four hands.

DUSSHALA

LANDAY FOR DOOMED SIBLINGS

We're all dying, less or more broken.
The sages say this is what it means to be human.

To be human, like runes on parchment:
to fade, to tear, to melt – and, sometimes, to be unmeant.

Unmeant blob of flesh, last orison –
I am both: lone daughter, postscript to a hundred sons.

The hundred sons, loved, beloved, all
accursed, destined to die; sludge and blood to be their pall.

No pall, no pyre, no funeral song.
They deserve more: once dead, even sinners should belong.

Some sinners. Flawed, for sure, all. Yet dear,
my brothers: Hastina's lights that wane; will disappear.

Each light I shall weep – weep and recite
their names, etch their voices on these woods, this wind, this night.

For their warts, voices, their nights, their loves,
all vanish – when dead, they'll know fame as hundred Kauravs.

Reduced to a number, a clan name.
That cannot be. They must be remembered. Mourned. Reclaimed.

First VIRJASA, my nearest sibling,
once the child who lassoed stars with Father's signet ring.
Strands of that wonder I hold within
the heart, candescent, clean, free from all sorrow and sin.

KUNDASHI, the one with a quarter-
moon on his cheek; earth and sky to his little daughter.

DIRGHABAHU, DIRGHAROMA, both
were melomaniacs – their aubades, the day's happiest troth.

MAHABAHU, we often forgot –
there's one like him in every clan, silent floe of thought.

ANAADHRISHYA, ALOLUPA and
ABHAYA breathed and lived as one, digits of a hand.

CHITRANGA commanded fealty.
With phoneme, frown and tread, he exuded royalty.

KAANCHANADHWAJA, folks often took
for gandharva: bewitching as midnight, tined as hook.

SAMA and SAHA wore summer's crest
in their eyes. The bards claimed their smiles ushered each harvest.
Siblings tend to discount each other's
charms, but even I saw beauty in these two brothers.

JALAGANDHA was clearly mortal.
But when he spoke, words seemed to unbolt heaven's portal.

DUSHPRADHARSHANA was not handsome.
But his heart, his giant heart, was worth a king's ransom.

DHRIDARATHASRAYA had fought hard
and long with his wayward locks, then went bald as reward.

You wouldn't spot DURMARSHANA – lithe
and small – in a crowd. But no target could miss his scythe.

SULOCHANA was a bully, though.
SARASANA too. Neither was good with sword or bow.

DUSSALA, DUSHKARNA, DURMUKHA,
savants, urged us all to forsake the path of duhkha.

Then VEERYAVAN, PRAMATHA, also
VIRAVI: once my heroes, slayers of infant woe.
They'd speared nightmares, the dark and dragons.
They'd made my childhood the brightest, blithest of seasons.

Like a mountain oak stood VIVITSU,
firm, tall and peaceful – rare was the battle he'd debut.

VIKARNA and KARNA, the kingdom's
moral hinge: cursed, the day our court expunged your anthems.

DUSSHASAN became a fearsome curse –
a raptor owned his heart. His malice signalled our hearse.

UPACHITRA and CHITRAKSHA swayed
easily – that infamous day, they joined the melee.

CHARUCHITHRA was more a cipher.
I never knew if he'd be tiger, steed or viper.

DURMADA and DURVIGHA abstained
from both sides till the war – they just craved a stable reign.

Far-sighted was our KUNDHABHEDI.
He'd warned Father of that blue krait, Maama Shakuni.
In vain, for Father never listened.
And Shakuni's pale nimbus ate and grew and glistened.

RAUDRAKARMA and VIRABAHU,
gentle scribes: both to their monikers remained untrue.

DURDHARSHA and CHITRAKUNDALA
spent their waking hours crafting intricate mandala.

Not SUBAHU nor DUSSAHA, who
only cared to hunt creatures that ran or swam or flew.

VIKTANA loved weapons. Not to kill
with, but to carve, forge and hone; the strength required, the skill.

URNANABHA and SUNABHA taught
soldiers to become arrows: straight lines, swift, light and taut.

UPANANDA cared deeply for joy,
not just his own, but all the people in his employ.

Sweet sorrow blooms each time memory
unearths pranksters KUNDADHARA, KRADHAN and KUNDI.
Their laughter spilled beyond palace walls –
fresh, vibrant laughter, now to be cradled by earth's caul.

While DHANURDHARA's banner stirred fear
in the sinews and hearts of warriors far and near.

AADITYAKETU, I never knew,
at least, not until I touched the shattered skies he drew.

SUVARCHA, though – also VATVEGA –
I could see through, whether quick hoax or ornate saga.

DURADHARA and SUHASTHA were
different: they studied scriptures, they spoke in a blur.

BHIMVIKRAMA while a gifted cook,
too, preferred – unlike his near-namesake – to devour books.

KAVACHI, UGRASAYI along
with SADAS forever stayed teens – they loved feeling wronged.

APRAMATHIN, though, was wise from day
one: he steered clear of the endless Pandav-Kaurav fray.
Now, alas, even he has no choice.
Each kin must take sides; no room is left for a sane voice.

VISHALAKSH, KUNDASAI, APARAJIT
and SENANI, great archers, deserve another myth.

UGRASEN busied himself without
fuss – healing souls and bodies maimed through war, fire and drought.

MAHODARA's talent never sought
acclaim. But when he danced, constellations were rewrought.

Our mahouts prized NAGAADAT dearly.
He could calm the deadliest beast with a caress, merely.

And DUSHPARAJAI was adored
by Nishadas: he'd soar with them till the ocean floor.

Grandsire Bheeshma disapproved of these
lowborn pursuits – and of CHITHRA, who grew shala trees.

Grandsire once had exiled BAHVASI
for mouthing strange, volcanic words like *democracy*.

But he never raised voice or eyebrow
the day DHRIDHAHASTHA slew a maid who did not bow.

Nor was UGRASRAVA reproved when
he razed a Kuru town: *Mistakes happen to all men.*

SUVARMA was hailed by the court for
banning fisher-folk from town – thus was varna restored.

Of all my brothers, AYOBAHU
alone asked if I wished to wed the King of Sindhu.

SATHYASANDHA, amidst all this roil,
became my comfort, my compass; he shone tall as foil.

JARASANDHA got away for some
time. In Hampi he learnt new tongues, and quaffed the humdrum.

DRIDASANDHA and ANUDARA
found harbour in their brides, doe-eyed twins from Sopara.
Their wives – Kriti and Saachi – well knew
the cost of war, one they'd hoped never again to view.

DURVIMOCHAN courted my husband's
niece. She died young – and that phantom love he would not rend.

VINDA and ANUVINDA, shameless
flirts, knew the name of every woman in the palace.

Our maids Mother kept safe from abuse,
so CHITRABANA went elsewhere to claim seigneur's dues.

BHIMVEGA had pined – little did we
know – for years, enamoured of a lissome nartaki.

SOMAKIRTI and PASHI remained
single – nuptial life, they professed, would drive them insane.

Grandsire spewed fire when SALAN explained
he liked men. Mother said: *Life is no sin when unfeigned.*

They all lost sleep over NISHANGI.
As teen, he'd run off with a bhang-eating yogini.

We had real misfits in the clan.
DRIDHAVARMA, poor soul, believed he was born a swan.
I recall the day that he – egged by
Bheema – near leapt off the turrets, certain he could fly.

Both frightened and repulsed me, as child,
till DRIDHAKSHATRA told me roses smelt fairest wild.
That those with whom you grow or belong
need not bear shades you'd choose, or the glow of evensong.

SUVARMA the SECOND loathed his name.
A priest's lapse: he'd had a hundred and one to declaim,

UGRAYUDHA and CHITHRAYUDHA
gained fame and fortune – across seven seas – as siddha.

CHITRAVARMA travelled far and wide,
then decided by which deity he would abide.

SUSHENA hailed Krishna as divine.
He said the Dark One would ravage all forces malign.

Balvardhan was a born agnostic.
Doubt was his faith, but he was intrigued by tantric.

Chitrakunda refused to worship
the gods. Anyone else would have been slain, at least whipped.
But Kund diffused charm in abundance.
Gods don't care for goodness, he'd quip without comeuppance.

All through, Bhimbala and Valaki –
devout, brave, gentle – stayed favourites of Ma Kunti.

Yuyutsu I cannot count among
kin: another mother he has, other heart and lung.

Nanda to Arjun was a dear friend.
Then the dice game and exile wreaked wounds that would not mend.

Sathwa and Nakul swore to sustain
their kinship till the end: some hearts will not be arraigned.

Vrindarak and Bheema were kindred
spirits since boyhood. Now Bheem's sworn to kill all hundred.
Vrindarak just asked it be rapid.
They both know oaths matter more in a war this sordid.

Suyodhan. Ô where would I begin?
Finest of kings, staunchest friend: made synonymous with sin.
Gentle brother, had you not fallen
prey to wrath and greed, Kuru'd stay more blithe than heaven.

I scatter their memories – this past
imperfect, yet glorious – lest they be named outcast.

Scatter their names, their light like fireflies
among a conference of birds who sieve truth from lies.

Birds who'll fly these truths – these tales – to times
and lands near and distant, so once more will sound their chimes.

While here, in Bhaarat, the bards will sing
only victors' odes – psalms on the lost dead don't greet spring.

ULUPI

THE CAPILLARIES OF COSMIC BODIES

Arjuna, I send you the son you've never seen:
our son, yes, your firstborn, Aravan. It will mean
nothing to you, his gentle name, I know. Nor mine,
perhaps – Ulupi, daughter of Kouravya, Queen

of the Naga. For names seldom count. To refine
your vision, recall Devprayag, the river shrine –
Ganga's cradle – you'd visited in your first golden
year of exile. Recall the naiad who'd entwined

her pulse and breath with your own, plunging nine frozen
leagues down – down, with you in her arms, your heart molten
with wonder, limbs cursives of sudden, mute delight –
to the netherworld, shimmering, aqueous glen

of the serpent kings, and frontier of heaven's might.
Recall how you had gazed, in the nacreous light,
at her speed, her allure, then begged to gain the same
mystic skills – to wage war underseas, to ignite

oceans with a single spell. Remembrance reclaims
you now, and oblivion blossoms into shame.
For though men of Kuru enjoy a history
of forgetting wives and lovers, to disclaim

a tutor – as I, who granted you victory
over seven worlds below earth – bodes misery,
moral ruin in your mind. But it scarce matters:
I've hardly pined that you expunged from memory

the mirrored blaze of my thighs and lips, or attar
from my rose! That night meant a quick, luscious patter
in both loins, nothing more – a night I had acquired
in return for the runes you needed to shatter

rival armies: your seed my teacher's fee, the fire
to forge my child. For it was not burning desire
that impelled my barter for coitus, you see,
but my clan's need for fresh warrior stock to sire

the next monarch. Yet our Elders first reproached me
for choosing an earthling, Indra's son and demi-
divine though you were; worse, Aravan had to face
down, when young and unknowing, the ignominy

of words like half-breed and mutt, for the human race
stays second-rate among serpents. But he embraced,
to our surprise, his father's blood with fiercer pride
in response, rising so tall and true that Disgrace –

who'd dogged his tread through childhood – fell by the wayside
and never caught up again. Staunchly has he tried
to be worthy of you. But more than the echo
of his sire – so much more – is this son who bestrides

seven spheres as numen, the camber of his bow
shaping earth's vault while his smile ushers tomorrow.
He is what matters, Prince: Aravan, beyond wrong
or crown; the future, which is not ours to forgo.

I knew it would kill, I knew the ache to belong
would send him here, to this crazed, dissonant swansong
of war – for sons will slash their lifelines for distant
fathers, to please kin who've disdained them all along

while mothers and lovers and life, in an instant,
are forsaken for combat, for the swift, brilliant
death or painless triumph they believe lies ahead.
Neither – they will find, alas – proves to be constant.

I'd graft Aravan to the ocean floor, embed
my son within deep murmurs of my heart, or spread
him amongst the farthest stars to keep him from harm,
if I could – but moths seek the flaming braided thread

for death, even when unlit. Wherein lie fire's charms,
Arjuna, what makes them yearn to drown in its arms?
I've mulled on that for long. I know what this portends,
but goddesses cannot mourn, nor raise an alarm.

I do not ask you to love him, nor to pretend.
Who can love on demand, even to make amends,
even one's own blood? And Aravan deserves more,
as soldier, as being: I ask that you extend

to my son the courtesy, the care you'd outpour
on an ally; the candour you'd unveil before
equals. Do hold his filial trust unbetrayed,
even the day you deflect his lifeblood, his core

to raze the foe, when war spreads from earth to invade
the skies, when the end crawls up, and its breath abrades
your spine. Grant him his lineage, complete with sheen:
watch him stroll towards death, his pulse the serenade.

KRISHNA

BLUEPRINT FOR A VICTORY

It's war we're waging. Look,
   Yuddhishtira, someone must die,
      must kill himself, and willingly, so
      we can prevail. Or a galaxy of dead
   eyes will be your only legacy
to this land, to this age.

Yuddhishtira, someone must die,
   your priest insists. It'll be amavasya
      in a day: Surya and Chandra are about
      to rise as one in the sky; Kali will crave
   a human sacrifice, from the perfect
warrior on the front. Then

someone, Yuddhishtira, must die
   tonight, before Duryodhana slays
      a white elephant to gratify the gods
         (and collects their choicest boons
   for victory). I can hoodwink the sun,
the moon – and most others – but

someone must die, Yuddhishtira,
   and remember, without pain, or wants
      unsated. Three warriors alone on our
      side can make the cut, their skins blessed
   with the ritual signs of sacrifice, all thirty-
two: Arjuna, Prince Aravan, and I.

Someone must die, Yuddhishtira,
    but not – you agree – your brother,
        Arjuna, commander of our army, star
          archer, and iris of your mother's
    eyes. But you needn't panic, for I
can take on the role, of that

someone, Yuddhishtira, who must die!
    Happily, since my death will bring
        you victory, pledge I gave to Draupadi.
          No, no, let me, cousin, for what is life
    but a garment to wear and discard?
You insist you won't let me be

someone who must die, Yuddhishtira,
    but it isn't such a big deal. All that
        matters in life is duty, and mine is clear:
          order in the world, at every cost, even
    of justice and integrity – order's the thing,
see, the recipe for empires, the reason

someone must die, Yuddhishtira,
    the reason countless others will
        also die, the reason you – and not
          your cousin Duryodhana – and yours
    must win this war, must inherit my
planet: for order and not revenge.

Yuddhishtira? Someone must die,
    but you understand why. There's no time
        to waffle or pine: if you won't let me, Aravan
          alone remains – your uncle Shalya would do
    but he fights now on the other side.
So what if the lad's an ally?

Someone must die, Yuddhishtira,
    and he didn't come to Kurukshetra
        for a party. Yes, he's keen on dying
            in battle, but a sacrifice will bring him
        greater glory – for once, it isn't a lie. I'll
    convince Aravan and his parents too.

Someone must die, Yuddhishtira,
    and Arjuna will have to bid his half-
        serpent son goodbye, but he never
            knew the boy, and this is a higher
        cause than family. Besides, he has
    other sons; but Ulupi won't agree

someone must die, Yuddhishtira,
    not when that someone to die
        is her only son, heir to her throne. Nor,
            though, will she deny Aravan his whims.
        So we have to ensure this is an end
    the boy desires. Not that easy, when

someone must die, Yuddhishtira.
    Convince Aravan he's the chosen
        one, marked by destiny, marked through
            his very body, proof irrefutable if
        proof ever there'd be of his being
    kalapalli, the one, the blessed

someone who must die. Yuddhishtira,
    we asked and here's Aravan's reply.
        You were right: he would prefer to die
            in battle, but he will comply. On
        condition, though, that he be wed –
    in word and truly in deed – first.

Someone must die, Yuddhishtira,
    yes, but not a virgin. Aravan
      asks to be deflowered tonight,
      or all offerings will be in vain.
    We asked and asked again, but
no woman agrees to marry

someone, Yuddhishtira, who must die
    on his wedding night. No woman
      wishes to be widowed quite so soon,
        nor gutted alive as sati. But if no such
    woman exists, I'll supply a bride. It is one
night's tale, not a lifetime affair. If

someone must die, Yuddhishtira,
    so must another be born, or remade.
      There will be a woman by twilight, for
      Aravan to wed and bed. You may be young,
    but you've still heard, I guess, of Mohini?
You can count on her to lie with him,

Yuddhishtira. Someone must die,
    must first sigh appeased, pleased. And hence
      I shall transform, unsheathe my female form:
      reap lush, tender breasts and fragrant hips,
    sate him with the velvet of my thighs and lips,
drown him in embrace all night long. For

someone must die, Yuddhishtira,
    and it is no sin to grant him this wish.
      If that, thereby, entails a change of sex,
      so be it. Why the horrified stare? If I can
    morph into boar and fish and man-lion
to save the world, why not a woman?

Somone must die, Yuddhishtira,
    and that someone deserves a wife to cry
        over his death, if just for half a day. Besides
        I've been Mohini once before, Enchantress
    no deity could ever resist, nor forget. If
the gods didn't mind, why should men,

Yuddhishtira? Someone must die,
    your flesh and blood, it transpires,
        to guarantee your conquest. And all you
        find awry in this carousal of bloodlust
    is that man will love man tonight? Ring
temple bells, garland weapons, and sing

instead, *Yuddhishtira: someone shall die.*

MOHINI

JEREMIAD FOR THE DEBRIS OF STARS

a curse
a curse   a curse
on you

a

curse
on you

a curse on
all of you
gods demons sovereigns
oceans planets mountains moon
fire earth   on all you
gaping
stars

a curse on creatures   a curse on all that rises
of the night   of day   that gleams that shades
on trees   on this air   that razes   that invades
a curse on all that
remains

For he breathes no more
aravan breathes no more no
more hears nor speaks no
more sings with the breeze no
more do his feet anchor the
earth no more do his cheeks
kiss the sun's roving fingers no
more does he taste the sandal the
musk of these breasts no more
does he savour nectar in the hollow
of a neck no no more no more will
his skin warm my skin shoulder to
instep no more will his hands map
the journey of filaments from navel to
pudendal cleft no more can he rest his
head between my legs no more his mouth no
more his manhood no more pulse no more
thought no more aravan

a
curse
on you

for he is no more aravan is no
more no more he is no more
than thirty-two slivers of flesh for
kali's tongue offering for pandava
victory no more than gashes
on a head a chest a belly nose
temple the point the sacred point
between eyebrows twin sets ripped
of earlobes lips knuckles elbows
wrists shoulders knees insteps
then ten neatly-sliced toes yes thirty-
two slivers of flesh that imbrue
the earth with geysers of unending
unfading ritual red while the rest the
rest will be fed to agni's hungry craw his
blazing crimson craw nape of neck and
clavicle ribcage breastbone gizzard spine
and sinew gullet and tongue and teeth
his burnished gaze his voice the river ripple
of his voice his smile his smile his smile the
colour of summer noon

a curse
a curse   a curse
on you

a curse on night on last night
heedless violet-skinned night
that sped towards dawn
flashing toe-rings and anklets
night that ended my heart
ended most of my life

a curse on kali a curse on
all heaven a curse on any god
that clamours offerings any
god that trades in blood and
breath for blessings a curse
on them all of them gods that
revel in bloody mayhem in
sacrifice a hundred curses

a curse on hastinapur a curse
on this feckless land on all its
kings on the ancient house
of kuru with its parricidal
kin a curse on bheeshma for
his dreadful vow on vyaasa
who kept bharata's line alive
a curse on dhritarashtra on
dead pandu on gandhari
and kunti and their many
murderous thoughtless good
deeds a curse

a curse a bigger a viler a direr curse
on those five pandava brothers
bastards all yuddhishtira the
pious eldest who sends his
children to die for a paltry
throne powerful bheem
who watched all this
injustice reign and
killed only his
cousins

the same curse dark and vile and dire
on duryodhana the cause of this
war on dushasana the next in
line evil disrober of women
and all ninety-eight siblings
jealous bitter blood to be
spilled on kurukshetra's
sacred earth sacred
only to brahmins
or the living

then arjuna oh
the bright peerless arjuna
precious to the gods arjuna
who fights behind krishna's shield
arjuna who let his son his firstborn
aravan take his place at kali's
altar bleating he is helpless
at every amoral turn

and a curse on you
ulupi mighty queen grieving mother
a curse on you for not keeping him
safe for not keeping aravan away
what use is free will if it fetters
breath if it smothers pulse so why
must mothers permit sons to follow
noxious fathers but what curse
could be worse than aching womb
than empty heart what curse of
mine could ever be worse ulupi

a curse
a curse   a curse
on us

on you krishna lord of fourteen worlds a curse a curse
the vilest of all curses on you on you for these gods these
demons sovereigns oceans planets mountains moons
for this fire this earth this heaven for all these gaping stars
a curse on you the foulest of curses krishna for spinning
this loathsome universe into light for this war that razes
countless men and beasts hope and goodness a war that
parches land and sea and sky the war that you willed into
being a curse on your dharma that changes shape and colour
and size to suit the wearer your mutant bootless justice and
your lethal cosmic song a curse a curse a curse on you for this
deadly master plan to ensure pandava victory the ruse to spare
your cherished arjuna a curse on you for contriving aravan's death and
a million curses I hurl at you krishna for transmuting into maiden
into mohini into me a curse for proffering this choiceless coupling
this heady grief a million curses for your power o god that creates god that
destroys god that forgets as gods so easily do

        a curse on me a curse on me for I live while aravan lies unmoving reduced
        to thirty-two slivers of flesh to geysers of unfading ritual red for while I
        breathe he can no more dream for I speak while his tongue is a mere blaze
        of flame for while I walk his legs are firewood on a pyre while I taste air he
        is just a name while I dance he is dead sacrifice a curse a curse on
        my breast-cloth his fingers can no more undo on my bracelets
        that will never mark his skin on my eyes for they behold aravan no more
        only carcass and bone a curse on this gaze whose lust can stir him no
        more on nails that will never graze his spine again hands that
        will not wind around his neck fingers that need never entangle
        his a curse on my breasts for they will blossom in his palms
        no more on my lost laughter that will not caress his lips again
        a curse a curse on this womb that never will bear his
        seed and watch it grow and one last vicious curse on
        my transient woman's soul that will forget aravan after
        this morning when it becomes male once more for
        krishna will not spare me a morsel of memory not
        the comfort of mourning nor the covenant of a
        married name

a curse
a curse   a curse
on me

SPOUSES, LOVERS

CONSTANCY V

What more is there to say we breathe we act we live until we die[8] there
will be more there may always be more more thought more hope more
prayer more pleas more planets and comets more orbits for moons more
oceans with mountains more scree more rage in the rivers more livid
fear more waves more trees more lore more birds more arms their feet
more beckoning shores and yet and yet and yet more is not enough never
nearly enough to hold this day in the heart of a palm to lull today to
safety to stillness for time does not snag between our lips for thought just
weighs a syllable for hope leaves no contrails for prayers deliquesce for
pleas leave no ashes for comets care little for you or me for orbits have no
desire for moons are lighted shadows for oceans cannot impale red stars
for no mountains could halt today for rivers will not rise to snare the
sun for trees hurl no branches to tangle the moon for birds will founder
and arms and legs do tire for no waves stifle divine decrees for the lore
always lies for the song must end for this day this one last day before
the battle must blaze white and die with its colours like hours falling
sideways shredding dry seas with rain staining indigo earth once again
for night flows like sand for night catches like wildfire for this night is
a beast three lungs two throats a belly with barbels but no eyes nor ears
and never skin its throats spewing anthems of unreason for this night
tonight churns living metal mineral souls old blood for the battle begins
in the night of our fears for all that is left for all that is left to sight to
claim to own is a distant shore of yesterday all that is left to touch to trace
to memorize is the tattoo of my breath on your brow for until we die we
live we love we kill and there is little more to say

SATYAVATI

XI. FAULT LINES

Listen. Listen, where do I begin? Or perhaps, should I wonder, how do I end? Isn't that the question? How do we all end? Sequestered in tombs, sailed – rotting – down rivers, strewn on high mountains as soot and cinders? If only it were that simple, that final. And then, some of us are made to live on as symbols. Made to walk on the roof of myth or history and slide off the rafters, in never-ending tendril. Made to repeat our errors and stories through perpetuity. Made to dwell in the past and the future while the present alone stays elusive, invisible. Such random, ominous thoughts and notions slid about my mind, like plates beneath the earth's crust: fault lines appeared, fractured, multiplied – and widened into seismic clefts. I clenched night, spinous, opalescent night, between my teeth. I heard the moon's jagged edges carve my throat, I sensed it wedged in the larynx. It felt like all the light from Gandhari's famous, shuttered eyes was caught in my gullet.

The journey seemed endless. The journey back to Hastina, it took three months, a week and two nights and swallowed several lives, human and animal. But I hardly noticed the dangers, the deterrents, only the delays. Those visions blitzed my night and day, not lucent and unambiguous as the first time, but chromatic, grotesque, a few all too recurrent. I saw a colossal, hideous lump of flesh egress from the loins of a woman, faceless in agony and shame. I saw the lump portioned into a hundred – then one more, though tiny – parts, stored in earthen jars by rough, efficient hands I knew at once – even in that nebulous, distant world – as those of my son Vyaasa. I saw the jars shake the palace walls, shake the earth with ululations; roil clouds and seas with unearthly thrums; saw the jars burst open to spill desolation, loud and clangourous, in the form of a hundred cherubs, soft and innocent. And I saw my grandson Pandu, flanked by two beauteous females – one childlike and blithe, the other intent – on a lush, high glade, far from court and capital, far from opulence but far from woebegone. I saw supernal beings descend from heaven and conjugate, first with the grey-eyed, pensive woman, then the younger one, while Pandu danced, danced in anticipation. The next instant I saw them flocked by five radiant sons, children who disgorged stone and metal, magma, meteors. I saw them all, palace-dwellers and woodlanders alike, transform; infants become rock warriors. I saw them whirlpool continents, wrack oceans; I saw them decapitate tens of thousands.

Listen. Listen, when we reached home and my eyes fell on Vyaasa's face, I knew no surprise at all. There he stood, now a wizened sage, but tall and contained, with none of the rampant whiskers and mane, nor the mercury of yore. *You returned, Mother, although you saw all the portents. I salute your sense of duty, your courage though not your lack of self-preservation.* Clearly, my son hadn't changed as much as his looks implied. And before I could respond, he continued, whether to himself or me I could not construe. *You saw it all in your visions. Yuddhishtira, Kunti's firstborn – fathered by Dharma, God of Death and Justice – was born some full moons ago. And Bheema – the second, this mighty one sired by Vayu, Lord of the Winds – will arrive before next spring. Yes, Mother, niyoga once more, at Pandu's insistence lest he die without offspring to perform the last rites and dispatch him to heaven. Though Kunti is more amenable to persuasion than your daughters-in-law were – and Madri will actually clamour for her turn. In Hastina, though, Dhritarashtra's rage knew no bounds on hearing of his nephew's birth. He declared Gandhari accursed and barren, though her belly – round as a melon – was full of his unborn children. He tupped and tupped again a dasi designated by his priests until she fell pregnant. Frantic and senseless in pain, Gandhari wrested aforesaid belly with an iron bar so she'd egest – but you've already seen that and the rest.*

Mother, I've just shattered that lump into many bits and nested them in urns with sacred oil and my benedictions. In nine months, Dhritarashtra and Gandhari will become parents to a full century of bairns. While Pandu will have three more scions attached to his name: Arjuna, born to Kunti from Indra, yes, the King of Gods himself; then, Nakula and Sahadeva, the fruit of Madri's tryst with the Ashwini Twins, those dashing godly physicians. Who could own a more refulgent litter! But prepare to mourn, Mother, prepare to mourn and never stop mourning. For Pandu will die before his youngest sons begin to speak, will die when he forgets the vile curse that hangs over his fate, will die from carnal bliss in Madri's arms. And she'll die too, unable to live with remorse, die leaving her two sons under Kunti's aegis. Kunti, ordered – by both late husband and clan shibboleth – to be mother and grandmother of monarchs. Kunti, who's always been more queen mother than either queen or mother; Kunti, who will strive – at all costs – to regain the throne for Pandu's firstborn. Kunti, who will return to Hastina, and unleash her half-divine progeny amidst a hundred Kaurava pigeons – pigeons who are no less raptors. Mother, come away with me, come away now. Do not stay to watch your great-grandchildren tear each other and the world apart, then drown it in haematic flood. This is a splendrous – if gruelling – epic to read or write, but not one you want to inhabit, Mother, no, not when the killers and the killed will all be your own sinew and blood.

Bewildered and distraught, I interrupted: *But surely no child is born evil, Vyaasa. Given the right care, with the right values, surely we can save them still. I cannot bear to surrender without trying. Nor to abide thoughtlessly by cosmic visions and rumour mills, be these sights so demonic.* Vyaasa's shoulders stooped at that, he bore the pain of centuries. *No, Mother, no child is born evil, on that we full agree. It is not evil itself that will plague our descendants, initially, but hate – almost the same thing in effect, alas, though not in cause: many good men hate, and will destroy wantonly in their hate, yet reject the notion of evil influencing decisions or actions. These children, Mother, are being brewed in hate, and steeped in it they will grow. How many hates will you battle? Assailed by all the colours and tones of hate in the universe will the Kurus be. Hate that will play every instrument to sound a symphony of doom across the firmament. So many rhythms and colours emanate from that hatred, Mother, our eyes and ears may crumble and desiccate at their advent. At the near beginning stands Amba's hate, a hate that consumes planets and stars and comets, that transcends, why, owns Time, hate that will resound as Bheeshma's nemesis: the warrior Shikhandi, soon to be born to Dhrupad – a king who will embrace hate as his lifelong consort – in the nearby land of Panchaal. Amba-Shikhandi who will transform from woman to man by the sheer might of her vengeance, who'll plague Bheeshma with the memory of desire and wrong until the day he shall perish. Add to this the silent, frightened loathing of Ambika and Ambalika that flowed, on leaving their latterly quietened souls, into Hastina's mud and rivers – and perhaps their children's blood.*

Or take Gandhari, whose wounds throb and bleed as unending righteousness, sainthood more virulent than any wickedness. Except the malignance of her brother, Shakuni, orphaned by Kuru forces and forced to watch a blind man wed his sister. Shakuni, who has sown – with quiet success – fear, distrust and wrath in Dhritarashtra's once loving heart. Shakuni, who will soon blueprint his hate onto his eldest nephew Suyodhana's being, will fill the boy's thoughts and deeds with venom to devastate this land. Then Kunti, with a hate birthed by that needless second wife Bheeshma bought to dispel the true rumours of Pandu's impotence. A hate alchemised into impermeable, unbending love for all five children, love that will impede all other love and light from reaching them, leaving wives and sons and lovers wounded by the wayside. You talk of values, Mother, of training their sights away from evil. But their future preceptor, Drona, their idol, their ideal, Drona, is a man honeycombed by hate – by his hostility to Dhrupad, the childhood playmate who wronged him grievously in later life. It shouldn't matter to us, Mother. But it will, for all his lessons, his guidance – on archery or governance, statecraft or gnosis – will be fuelled by this hate. And hate is the guru dakshina he will exact from his students: he will demand they subjugate Dhrupad and annexe Panchaal. A hate that will spawn more hate, for Dhrupad will then seek, and obtain, vengeance from heaven – this is a spiral that just will not abate. How can you combat these many legions of hate, Mother?

Listen. Strips of thought glided and spooled in my head, thoughts that spiralled, thoughts that undid me even as he spoke. I could hear truth, many-armed, cruel-tongued, singing through Vyaasa's voice, truth that would not be interred. But why, I asked in despair, could he not obviate the course of history with all his astral powers, why did he not erase this hate with his pen that shapes the story? My son's voice was suffused with the fatigue of enlightenment. *Mother, I cannot invent*

*the story. The story invented itself, invented you
and me. I can merely act as channel, as implement.
I am assigned to circulate the epic in the world but I
could not change a time of birth or the placement of
a line if I tried: to obliterate or dilute this explosion
of kinetic hate is beyond my ken. It haunts me night
and day, blessed by celestial insight though I am.
Illumination and wisdom do not always bring
detachment. I miss my earlier, imperious self,
Mother: half-knowledge brought such certainty. I
am sick of knowing, of seeing so much – it makes
me unsure, almost tremulous.*

*You, Mother, are fraught since you had those
visions – and you did not even know what they all
meant. I do. Even as I moulded the many fragments
of Gandhari's womb, I could see – ô, with blinding
clarity – the fate of each of those children. Bright
Vikarna, wise Dusshala, brave Suyodhana... I
could see their blood-soaked destinies as though
they were already legend. I see all the time, for it must
be written, and each vision scars my mind, leaves
nerves and muscles mangled. I see Kunti's return
to Hastina with her five sons, the terror Shakuni
will then stoke in Dhritarashtra's sightless heart,
and worse, in Suyodhana's sighted one. I see young
Bheema break his cousins' bones as recreation,
torment them generously through each waking
moment. I see their wounds swell and fester with
new hate. I see Duryodhan – for Suyodhana's hate
will colour him with malevolence and bequeath
on him this new, vicious name – poison Bheema's
plate with nightshade, bind the senseless boy with
his own raiment and tip him into the Ganga to*

die. I see Arjuna and his brothers – arrogant in their kshatriya breeding, intolerant of lesser-born beings – ridicule brilliant, noble Karna for his suta blood before the eyes of all Hastinapur.

I see the birth of more hate, hate distilled from injustice, hate between brothers, for Karna is Kunti's son from the Sun God, born well before she wedded Pandu – though Kunti alone knows the secret of his bloodline and she will not tell her other sons, silence that will engender a lifetime of obdurate, vicious dislike. I see Shakuni and Duryodhan plot to kill the Pandava clan, to burn them alive in a lac palace far away from home. I see, too, Kunti place six Nishada innocents in their stead as victims – the lives, yes, of lesser-born men will never count for our descendants. You and I too, Mother, would also be lesser-born beings in Pandava eyes, the thought often crosses my mind. I see much that falls on my vision as a rain of flame. I see Draupadi – luminous, fiery Draupadi, our cherished bride – near disrobed in Hastina's royal assembly; I see her stand, breasts blushing, blood racing from her thighs to hide within the earth while her husbands look on, impuissant. I see her curse – lethal, resonant – brand every ogling Kuru male in court; I see the words strike and truncate their lifelines, forked lightning once again. I see more. I see valiant Bheeshma suddenly turn corporeal, I see him transpierced by a bed of arrows, blood – in just-awakened glee – rushing across a marmoreal chest, fresh scars puckering lips on arms and legs. I see battalions of men and horses and elephants destroyed by single astras, entire families sent spinning into the void. I see the young die, mutilated, before tasting the colours of life.

But war is sometimes not the worst event, Mother: it just magnifies the evil men commit at other times. I see love discarded, over and over, by the Pandavas – discarded thoughtlessly and retrieved only for functionality. The love of good women – a palimpsest, the list of names long: Hidimbi, Bheema's wife, the eldest Pandava bride; Ulupi and Chitrangada, queens both, whom Arjuna meets and forgets after nights of passion and procreation. And their many official wives, none allowed to accompany the Pandavas – not in exile, nor to heaven. All except Draupadi, who will be paid for her constancy with her husbands' desertion both in dishonour and in death. And so much worse are the rewards to be meted on their sons, Mother. Ghatotkacha – the Pandava firstborn, half-rakshasa, half-human, Bheema's son from Hidimbi, forgotten until the land of adversity – will be deployed as shield to deflect the astra Karna sends to slay Arjuna. Or Aravan, Arjuna's son from Ulupi, who will be asked by his fathers to kill himself – human sacrifice to Kali – to ensure Pandava victory. Even Abhimanyu, the jewel in the Pandava crown, will die in his uncles' stead, though this murder, at least, will not be intended. What kind of progeny do we spawn, Mother? I have no answers, though write all this, every account of thought and action, intent and reaction, I must. For I am made up of letters: my skeleton, musculature and blood. The skin, the skin

*is pure memory – of past and future – and I would
erase it if I could. But I cannot, for write I must.
Come away with me, Mother. Come away now.
There is no more you can do for this land, this clan.*

Listen. Listen, the night was damp with unspilled
blood, the sky hung low, clouds of unshed tears
dragging it to earth. I could sense the impending
meltdown of this world; I could hear its funeral
rites behind the frenzied symphony now ringing
in my ears for three months, a week and two
nights. I could hear the birth of mayhem, feel
its atavistic pulse and I knew everything my
son described was about to happen, had already
begun – some in other lands, near and distant.
It was time to leave. But there remained one last
rite to be performed. *I will come,* I said to Vyaasa,
*but first I must bid good-bye to Bheeshma, noblest
of adversaries, steadiest of allies. Mine is an act of
abandonment, even though you state otherwise:
for Bheeshma is a man who does not understand
– nor recognise – hate, although there is much
he, too, generates. I do, I grew up wearing hate's
mantle for many years, though I learnt to shed
that carapace a long while ago. Bheeshma will be
helpless before its viscous, implacable flow. Let me
warn him before I go.* There was much I had to
tell him. Bheeshma, my stepson, my companion,
would have to learn – and learn fast – about old
hate, descended from heavens, leavened on this
land. Old hate, diffused through blood and womb
and semen. Old hate that I too begat, old hate
bequeathed and bartered, won in battle, given
as bride-price, hate that would blight at least six

generations of this clan, deforming husbands, grandsons, aunts and nephews, brides and celibates, hate that scarred every soul, even this baseborn sainted bard. Vyaasa, my lone living son Vyaasa, who had been given the words to hymn this story across millennia while birth and death and love and youth would jostle for place, while hate, old hate, would spore and multiply.

For Kurukshetra
is a ploy: men can create
mayhem in heaven.

UTTARAA

I. LIFE SENTENCES

The sky will not be sky again. It is dead
skin split open, drained of all music and blood.
Monarchs, ministers, nations, elders, fathers:
it will not be the same, the world you now own.
This I promise. You will never hear day break
into mute lucent song, never taste colour

again. Slivers of our trust will discolour
your waking hours; the screaming eyes of my dead,
all eight million, will plunder sleep; their broken
dreams – aged sixteen, lusty, loud – dance in bloodied
feet at the Council of Kings, dance ownership
of your crown. But, dharma, you state, must father

martyrs to save planets. Why then, Our Father
Who Stays Alive, why bring us new, colourful
balloons – faith, hope, freedom? Why brand us your own,
made in your image? What we are is deadly
disposable spawn, born benign (not bloodless,
imperfectly designed) then programmed to break

enemy battalions, smash unbreakable
armoured discs and self-combust for fatherly
glory. Yes, your dharma is a bloodthirsty
beast, a god decked in the primary colours
of dystopia: rusty, fetid, undead.
Rulers in righteous armour, you will not own

to filicide, nor bare the hands that disowned
your scions in their last hours. I must now break
away from your empire, shed this deadening

white guilt, end all myths on you, Founding Fathers,
and speak, speak, speak till memory brings colour
back to earth's cheek and she rises, sparing blood

in torrents. But hate, once seeped into bloodstreams,
is an abiding love: it already owns
today and tomorrow. Revenge will colour
our future in shadows and ancient heartbreak,
the terminal kind, for mothers and fathers.
And I, for all my foresight, will count the dead

again with deadpan voice and bloodstained fingers;
will seek father figures for my sons to own,
ones who teach them to break and decolour life.

II. TO ABHIMANYU: MEMORABILIA

I have so little to keep, to hold, of you,
they mourn, your kith and mine. True and untrue,
I should say, for memories run in my veins,
the dreams I dream are yours that spilled and stained
shared silken quilts and nights like auroral dew.

And when the taste of your tongue – nutmeg brewed
with lust – still teases my mouth, when your heart through
my beat does echo yet, this last terrain
I have. So little

it seems to those who never drowned in the blue-
black sludge of grief and rage, who never knew
this fetid pain, nor pursued ghosts to stay sane.
But our child within, future ghost who'll reign
to rage and revenge, is one more you of who
I'll have so little.

III. NOTE TO THE UNBORN CHILD

They will tell you he was a hero, child: your
father, my husband. They will swear he lived
a glorious death: swift and valorous, the royal
path to heaven on gilded chariot driven by gods
themselves. Abhimanyu: martyr, maharathi –
ace warrior, champion archer – hailed, in awe
and fear, as Indra, as Yama, at once lifesaver,
demolisher, and – variously – sheet lightning,
ancient umbra, supernova, annihilator
of aksauhinis, elephants, evil ambition. They will
sing of how he wrecked the padmavyuha, lotus
phalanx of doom, defanged its deadly petals,
smashed the spinning, hungry hub of a pistil,
strewing armed enemy forces as so many spores
until seven Kaurav generals – all routed in ones
and twos – girdled him in concert like a grist
of killer bees, stung from behind and smote
his breath in one fell swoop.

> *Choose, child, while still unborn; choose, for we*
> *no longer can, choose to remain free.*

His breath in one fell swoop, they will say
that's how it happened: blood-libation, liberation.
But the dead have no songs, child. No melodies
for regret or pain or pride. It is we that find and feed
them the songs, the words, rhythm, cadence,
refrain; we that redye the moments, each one;
friend, foe and father, grandfather god, doting
dowager, uncle-emperor, courtiers, seers, other
faded maws that scurry to rework histories,

so you will learn and hold as truth a thousand
staves of what you never saw nor heard while nested
in soft caul. So you will repeat what, when,
where and why, the why, yes, why your father –
land, pater, patria, one and many, heir to Kuru-
Vrishni glory – vanished in this giant playground
of carnage, of blocs, of left and right or east and west
or wrong and right, Krishna's right, always right
by name and number, faith and tongue.

> Choose, child, while still unborn; choose, for we
> no longer can, choose to remain free.

By name and number, faith and tongue, I cannot
swear, but no path, no gilded chariots, no gods
do I see. I see scattered your father's brains, ruddy
pomegranates glistening through churned slush; see
his gaze – my husband's gaze, the gaze that heralds
my night, my day – transpierced, dark grapes that imprint
earth; see traces of his smile in a torn cheek, in slivered
jawbone; see entrails undone, crushed beneath a dozen
armoured wheels; see bubbles of scarlet last breath
straining – still – to rise from severed neck towards
a cloven head: these lungs wish to live. With more speed
and mercy did Death seize sweet Lakshmana, the cousin
– once playmate – Abhimanyu killed: he slumps, speared
through throat and mast. An arm lies farther, my husband's
or a nameless, lost limb? Too much mud, too much blood,
too much flesh has flowed to read the palm, to know his touch
again but this is mine, the pulse of ruby on a finger, placed
last spring, the day our hands were interlocked.

Choose, child, while still unborn; choose, for we
no longer can, choose to remain free.

Last spring, the day our lives were interlocked, bards
from eight lands crooned of a match made in heaven.
More lies, child, now set to music: we were made for a war
alliance; sheer expedience, the vajra wedding
band to join Matsya and Kuru lands, fuse our clout
to their repute. A dowry of divine pedigree, a sea
of cavalry, prize warriors, and a seat in royal heaven.
For that, if need be, our kin would have married
their children off to a banyan tree. These matches made
in heaven, the bards never sing, are just tinder
for preordained pyre. But even sticks may brush, may
nestle, may intertwine. So it came to be: he wished
to build, not blaze, your father, the crown prince. For some
thing – not quite trust, nor truly love – happened, something
like life, undesigned. The notion of future, earth's gift
to our sixteenth year – the first, and only, summer
together – that swelled and curved to tempt him:
a curled up, compact quarter-moon in me.

Choose, child, while still unborn; choose, for we
no longer can, choose to remain free.

That curled up, compact quarter-moon in me,
the idea of you, drew him beyond right, might,
duty, loyalty – the alphabet he'd been given
to learn – towards other words and whims, call
them joy, permanency. But happy warriors, or
hopeful ones, are not good currency. Heroes
are dearest when dead, Krishna knows, flammable
fodder for survivors' guilt, rage, brutality. And what

better to stoke Arjuna's murderous frenzy than his
betrayed, butchered firstborn? The Kaurav cousins
crushed your father's skull, child, killed him when
unarmed, outnumbered, and despoiled the corpse.
But it is Krishna – best-loved uncle, guardian, the one named
divine, the same Krishna – that sent him to slaughter, one more
oblation to his famished earth. He was a son, Abhimanyu,
nephew, Kuru prince, brave, loyal, foolishly so; bravely, loyally
has he gone to his end. Here he lies, he that most wished to be
not hero – this, they will not tell you, child – but father.

KUNTI

OSSATURE OF MATERNAL
CONQUEST & REIGN

No mother can ever love each of her sons
alike. You should know, Draupadi, you who own
two five-chambered hearts, the smaller for your sons,
the first for husbands. Yes, Karna is my son,
my firstborn, forged as a shaft of living light –
rare, brilliant – but an accident, a son
I neither desired nor envisioned, the son
born of an unsought boon, arcane spell that moved
from a sage's lips to mine: power to move
much more than mountains or oceans – for a son
from a god could rule creation, etch your name
on myth and history, get planets renamed.

Draupadi, you ask why I left him unnamed
all these years, why I never hailed him, my son
Karna, as mine: Karna the fulgent, the name
any parent would rejoice, would vie, to name
as theirs. No, I never proclaimed him my own,
though not because he's baseborn, unnameable,
as the bards will soon sing. For who would not name
the scion of Surya, the Sun God who lights
the world? Vyaasa too, esteemed sage, alighted
out of wedlock – yet his mother takes his name
with joy and pride. Karna was an unplanned move:
at first, that enjoined silence. Too young, too moved,

was I to resist the Sun God. When he moved
towards me, eyes locking mine, I blazed; nameless
flames of purple and copper and crimson moved
through veins, our limbs dissolved, my womb glowed. Life moved

between our thighs, taut and sinuous. But sons,
like pleasure, should serve a purpose: I had moved
Karna from my sphere for I saw none, moving
swiftly before my faithless heart could disown
good sense. I sailed the child away from his own
kismat, down Ganga's arms – first having removed
all signs of kinship, save his father's lighted
armour and earrings, bequest to save, to light,

his life. Years later, when his fearsome skills lit
up Hastina's skies, I knew at once: he moved
in cursives, he quelled like a god, and the light
from his earrings drowned midnight. But aurous light
is too firm, too pure to rule the realm – namely,
not in suta-breeding lies his flaw, backlit
that day by brilliance; no, it is lightness
Karna lacks. A mother needs most from her son
compliance, chiefly to reign – the perfect son
for that is Yuddhishtir, well-trained, just half-lit
by resolve. Were I now, in public, to own
Karna, none of my sons, Child, would ever own

Kuru: Karna would crown Duryodhan owner
of earth, cede this war unfought, all to highlight
his friend's birthright. I'd rather sever my own
breath first! And hence I met him in stealth: I owned
the truth, he learnt we're kin. For now when he moves
in battle, he'll know that his siblings, his own
blood, face him; know either victory is owned
by fratricide. Arjun is the only name
he'll not spare – for their rivalry has been named
by heaven, he says; they'll duel till death owns
one, that is written. But I'll still have five sons,
when war ends, he swears. Who that last living son

will be rests on who can best perform a son's
role, Karna or Arjun, who's armed in his own
innocence; Arjun, whose arrows will delight
to greet his foe while sorrow mires Karna's moves.
A hero bears no shame, no grace, just his name.

VRISHALI

TESTAMENT:
VRISHALI WITH DURYODHANA

He is dead. Karna is dead, I
fear, for blood shrouds the moon, the stars
and your eyes. For light dies. For air
bruises my breath (thorns bloom in these
breasts). For words drown in your throat, King:
silence vanishes tomorrow.

He is dead – he must be – for why
else would a king arrest the war,
forsake field and forces, repair
to our doorstep, sink to his knees,
bareheaded, bereft, unspeaking,
and lay at my feet this mighty bow?

He **is** dead, yes – Vijaya, my
husband's bow, would never stray far
from Karna's flank, never forswear
its master's hands, unless he ceased –
the truth screams through bowstrings – breathing.
O King, speak – unleash – your sorrow,

roar: *He is dead!* O Sun, deny
no more your wretched heart: blaze, char
this world of unending despair.
Let nothing rest, no birds, no bees,
no gods, no human beasts. Nothing
but grieving clouds who should echo

He is dead. He, who'd defy
gods in their heaven, who could mar

the pride of monarchs, who had dared
reshape caste's vile coil, could not freeze
Yama's gross tread. Yet, would Death's sting
be mild, for so doomed a hero?

Dead. King, he saw, today he'd die
at Partha's hands; his lifeline scarred
mortally by the age-old glare
of brahmin curses, pre-deceased
by eight cherished sons – his sole sling
your trust, brace to spine and marrow.

He's dead now. And I must untie
the sightless mesh of his bizarre
birth and bloodline – did Bheeshma share
these stories? They sought to appease
him, after a lifetime's shaming
and defaming: this, you must know

now he is dead. Kunti came, cried,
begged him, once and again, to war
for the Pandavas, as the heir,
as her firstborn. By sun and seas,
by earth he swore, to one sibling –
just one king – his soul he'd bestow

till he's dead: you. Karna's reply
never faltered. He and you *are*
brothers, to Krishna he'd declared,
more brothers, more braided than trees
to earth. Krishna, who'd barter king-
ship and queen for Karna's arrows,

cheers he is dead. They deify
Krishna – the peacenik; Avatar

of Ruin is how I'd declare
such a blackguard. Karna's last pleas –
the time to free his wheel, to string
the bow, to rise – he spurned, bellowed,

He should be dead! Partha complied,
and tore that dear neck – a jaguar
slew the lion king in a snare.
Partha, I'll forgive: a reprise
of his son's slaughter was his spring;
Karna among those who'd wallowed

as the boy dropped dead, felled in sly
blitz. No, dharma left our durbar
an age ago. King, you're aware
of the sins, of rights and realms seized,
of women debased. Shadows sing
long, once breaths still and eyes hollow.

He is dead. End the battle cry,
King. Let blood from his jugular
cleanse your heart of anger, repair
your pain. It was his last dream: please
his soul, end the fratricide. Ring
out the war, let the hatred go –

for he is dead. Only the sky
remains untarnished, a vast jar
of sleeping ash. No, you'll not spare
the few living? You'll not release
peace from prison? You'll let loathing
prevail. Yes, words all sound shallow

when he lies dead. Aims and thoughts dry.
Your sole relief is arms that spar –

he'd comprehend. His love, his care
for you, King, never showed a crease
through the years; friendship abiding
beyond virtue, vice, overthrow.

Dead, still young. But he'd justify
his choice, each time, of side and tsar.
At first, I warned him to beware
of you – near-jealous, in unease
at whispers of star-crossed bonding.
Then I learnt how you bade him grow.

He is dead now. But he was nigh
unalive till you met, debarred
from his own brilliance; a wild flare
doused by old moths, those gurus leased
by courts. You saw a rare being,
crowned him – then basked in mirrored glow!

For till he fell dead, tall did fly
the Kuru flag, and from afar
and near came kings, ready to swear
allegiance, over eastern seas
and northern peaks. Pride, belonging –
he brought them home from you. And though

he may be dead, love will belie
mortal blood. Keep your heart ajar,
O King, for blessings unaware.
Now, it is time. You vowed to ease
my loss: so silence my paling
pulse and voice. Light one more arrow,

for the dead. I watched eight sons die,
brothers too, on the abattoir

that's Kurukshetra. In your care,
I leave our youngest: he still sees
life as a land worth exploring.
For mother's joys I must forgo –

Karna is dead. My troth I'd tied
to his breath. You aligned our stars
in life, long ago, King. Prepare
to merge our bones this time. The breeze
shall strew our ashes – hand nothing
to new kin. Set our pyre aglow.

BHANUMATI

AMARANTH

For tonight, dearest heart, Time has fled the battlefield,
ashen, unable: the abyss stands unsealed.

ᥫ᦮

For tonight dharma ripped out its three gagging, screaming
eyes, then slit its voice – now sutra just means string.

ᥫ᦮

For tonight prayers cower in shame and all gods flee.
Like widows, words weep: shed sound, try not to be.

ᥫ᦮

For tonight the sky, it prowls: a mute, livid monster
mouth gorging flesh and future, both imposters.

ᥫ᦮

For tonight the earth is a vast, unending sigh.
Grief stains air verdigris; rivers putrefy.

ᥫ᦮

For tonight the moon moves as a gibbous smear of blood,
dried blood, blood that bodes a chthonic flash flood.

ᥫ᦮

For tonight the sun drips black, deliquesces, as do
the stars; both sea and sky turn granite anew.

※

For tonight, they tell me, you are gone, dearest, gone and
dead. "Dead," they thunder, "dead," so I'll understand.

※

For tonight you become silence and smoke, dearest, ground
bone, oil, sandalwood, ash – a king by fire crowned.

SPOUSES, LOVERS

CONSTANCY VI

Before god
Before the dead
Before children
Before a world
Dance.

Before the sea drowns
Before clouds conflagrate
Before the phoenix drops
Before thorns flower
Write.

Before you leave
Before I lose
Before it rives
Before they blaze
Ravel.

Before you leave home, banished to a land named Alone
Before I lose my voice – voice that will roam spheres seeking yours
Before a border rives language from love, marrow and bone
Before words blaze through veins in jagged tongues of fire
Ravel wild cursives from a pledge
    Retrieve its letters – vowels, abjads and all
        Send them to safety, from lip to lip to heart and lung.

Before the sea drowns, gills clogged by a reign of blood
Before clouds conflagrate, scorch the seasons, rain dark light
Before the phoenix drops her song, sealing the casement to dawn
Before thorns flower in bronchioles and branches crowd airways
Write it all – little stories, giant histories, a few myths
    Tie them to cottonseeds, so they fall in distant hands
        Etch a copy on memory's palms: call it the human crease.

Before god dies, smile trampled, a thousand arms crushed underfoot
Before the dead return like moonlight, trailing white ash and regrets
Before children swap marbles for slugs and swallow darkness at meals
Before a world of straight lines and ironclad right owns your eyes
Dance, dance on vanishing shores between night and half-light
    Return, return to nest like stacked spoons, lock chest with spine
        Twine hip and thigh, knit ten fingers, purl the lips – once more

        Before the battle.

PADATI

II. The Son

PAWN TALK:
BENEATH THE MUSIC

There is   no Kurukshetra   Father

   No stair   nor   skyway to heaven   no winged

     chariots   for warriors   No heaven either

      No gentle north Father   no west   nor   east

        exists   No   no south   lined by Khandava

         lush Khandava   razed of blade   and beast

      an aeon ago   with Arjuna's   bow   stringed

    in royal greed   No centre Father   no silken

periphery   with maiden rivers   that ringed

    a sacred strand   sculpted by the hand   of Shiva

      No Shiva   Father   no devas even   just endless

       oceans of flesh   the sky a maw   spewing lava

     and pitch   juddering   drowning   earth below   a broken

    collar-bone of moon above   and   eyes   eyes   eyes

everywhere   thousands   riven   stricken

lost   and smashed   and   open   blind and bloodless

Eyes   Father   that need   no ballads   nor bards

to multiply   eyes that offer   no more redress

crushed pearls   on the chaplet of wise   men's lies

eyes that swear   I will   soon be   one of their kind

eyes that meld   into rubble and mulch   while trust dies

Trust   and   hope   and   fraternity   wretched shards

of humanity   all dead   Father   seeking that battlefield

where war was sacrament   where no chieftains   charred

soldiers with winged   astras and no kings   shattered minds

and lungs with toxins   Bheeshma   Father   the first

to break   his own vajra-bond   swiftly consigned

the rules of dharma yuddha   to myth and flame and congealed

the breath   of tens of thousands   mounts-musicians-messengers-men

Vaishya-Shudra-Mahar-Shanar-Kshatriya   When it came to carnage he repealed

caste and station   quaffed them all   though the lowest were dispersed

foremost   of course   to Yama's land   followed   by the Eight

Virtues Yes Satya-Daya-Daan-Suchi-Kshama-and-more all submersed this time   by Yuddhishtira   For Father   it is true   even

the noblest of kings   do sin   I saw the great Pandava skive

a sarathi in his seat   and slash   his horses   a fit of sullen

rage   when he could not rout the man's master   Late now   too late

Father   much   too late   to retreat-protest-berate   this was never

my battle and I will die for others' vows and dreams for yet another potentate

and so do a few   hundred thousand men   chests ablaze   a naïve

untimely   unremembered   bloom of Ashoka flowers   To die

forgotten is to die twice oblivion the final demise   we won't survive

No meridians no memorials just distance and the dead to sever

then swallow   the horizon   gorge the sun   it won't be long

now Father   before daylight leaves my eyes   I hear night   whisper

travelling northward   from the chest   what she thinks   a lullaby

travelling through spine sinew and nerve into lung and tongue and skin

Sludge covers   my eyes Father   or is that the hue   of a chagrined sky

Soon there'll be no variance   between soil and skin   both throng

me like a shroud though my flesh scalds and the soil stings with cold

Memory seeps   through torn veins   I begin   to unbelong from this self   from you   from the men who were mine   like kin

I used to know   Father   used to know   all   my peers

their voices   their names   Shibi there   the eye   of a javelin

caught his   smote him   burst the iris   spurting   dark gold

on eager earth   I used to know   his name too   the one fallen beside

me   an arm crushed   to unwilled clay   both legs further   rolled

further away   dragged beneath   his general's chariot wheels   a blear

in claret   the arc of betrayal   on hard ground   and him there

with an arrow twined   through the ribcage   next to the heart   as near

nearer than   a lover's beat   Satya Jaya Jeeva   the names collide

names and tones and functions   padati sarathi sainik rathi remember

them for me Father   The dead all look the same   no tones no pride

no traits no whims no gait   to call our own   save this one ware

For we cannot clamour   till   we are claimed   the names remain

our sole archives burn our spears our lances our shields but swear

you will chant the names of the faceless dead like a prayer Father

And await the day when you no more need righteous warfare nor heroes

No deadly belief no divine stairs no hereafter no Kurukshetra either

NOTES

1. A response to Vyaasa's description in Peter Brook's *Mahabharata*.

2. The 'Begin' refrains are variations inspired by Eva Recacha's 2011 dance trio *Begin to Begin*.

3. I. Blood Moon Rising: Poorna With Vyaasa

   This poem is a glosa that was built around the opening stanza from renowned poet and lyricist Gulzar's song *Naam Adaa Likhna* from Yahaan (2005). Here is the stanza taken as cabeza, with a rough translation below. Each stanza of 'Blood Moon Rising' 'glosses' on the corresponding line in the cabeza, that is, incorporates it as its tenth line.

   पूछे जो कोई मेरी निशानी, रंग हिना लिखना
   गोरे बदन पे ऊँगली से मेरा नाम अदा लिखना
   कभी कभी आस पास चाँद रहता है
   कभी कभी आस पास शाम रहती है
   आओ ना आओ ना झेलम में बह लेंगे
   वादी के मौसम भी इक दिन तो बदलेंगे

   Should anyone ask for my keepsake, my sign,
   write the colour henna, sign the name grace
   with your finger on my fair body.
   Now and then, the moon dwells here.
   Now and then, it is gloaming.
   Yes, come. Come, let us flow away in the Jhelum.
   The seasons in the valley will change too one day.

4. II. Poorna to Satyavati: The Handmaiden's Grail

   This poem, too, is a glosa. This time, the cabeza is taken from lyricist Niranjan Iyengar's opening stanza for *Ek Ghadi* from the film *D-Day* (2013). The stanza and its rough translation follow.

एक घड़ी और ठहर के जां बाकी है
तेरे लब पे मेरे होने का निशां बाकी है
शब के चेहरे पे चढ़ा रंग सवेरे का तो क्या
ढलते ख्वाबों में अभी अपना जहां बाकी हैं
एक घड़ी और ठहर के जां बाकी है

Stay a little longer, for life still remains.
Your lips still bear traces of my being.
Why care if dawn's colours suffuse the face of night?
Our world still survives within waning dreams.
Stay a little longer, for life still remains.

5. Riffed on a phrase from Kiran Nagarkar's *Bedtime Story*: 'This kingdom is ours. Its people are ours.'

6. Kunti's dialogue from the 1965 film *Mahabharat*, directed by Babubhai Mistri.

7. Regional term for the Pleiades.

8. A riff on a phrase from Salman Rushdie's memoir, *Joseph Anton*: 'you must live till you die', itself inspired by a sentence in Joseph Conrad's *The Nigger of the 'Narcissus'*.

REFERENCES

BIBLIOGRAPHY

Arni, Samhita. *The Mahabarata – a child's view –* (Tara Books, 1996).

Atwood, Margaret. *The Penelopiad* (Canongate Books Ltd, 2006).

Badrinath, Chaturvedi. *The Women of the Mahabharata: The Question of Truth* (Orient Longman Private Limited, 2008).

Balakrishnan, P.K. *Ini Njan Urangatte* (D.C. Books, 1973).

Banker, Ashok. *The Forest of Stories: Mahabharata Series Book One* (Westland Ltd, 2012).

Bhasa & (trans.) Iyer, G.S. *Complete Works* (D C Books, 2013).

Bhattacharya, Pradip. *Pancha-Kanya: the Five Virgins of Indian Epics* (Writers Workshop, 2005).

Bhyrappa, S.L. *Parva* (Sahitya Akademi, 1994).

Byatt, A.S. *Ragnarok: The End of the Gods* (Canongate Books Ltd, 2012).

Calasso, Roberto and (trans.) Parks, Tim. *Ka* (Jonathan Cape, 1998).

Das, Gurcharan. *The Difficulty of Being Good: On the Subtle Art of Dharma* (Penguin Books India, 2009).

Deb, Sandipan. *The Last War* (Pan MacMillan, 2013).

Debroy, Bibek (trans.). *The Mahabharata, Vol. 1-8* (Penguin Books, 2010-14).

Devi, Mahaswata & (trans.) Katyal, Anjum. *After Kurukshetra* (Seagull Books, 2005).

Divakaruni, Chitra Banerjee. *Palace of Illusions* (Doubleday, 2008).

Doniger, Wendy (trans. & intr.). *Hindu Myths* (Penguin Group, 1975).

Doniger, Wendy. *War and Peace in the Bhagavad Gita* (The New York Review of Books, Dec 2014).

Gardner, John & Maier, John (translators). *Gilgamesh* (Vintage Books, 1985).

Hiltebeitel, Alf. *The Cult of Draupadi, 1 Mythologies: From Gingee to Kuruksetra* (Motilal Banarsidass Private Limited, 1991).

Kalidasa & (trans.) Heifetz, Hank. *Kumarasambhavam: The Origin of the Young God* (Penguin Books India, 2014).

Kané, Kavita. *Karna's Wife: The Outcast's Queen* (Rupa & Co, 2013).

Karve, Iravati. *Yuganta: The End of an Epoch* (Sangam Books, 1974).

Kolatkar, Arun. *Sarpa Satra* (Pras Prakashan, 2004).

Komarraju, Sharath. *The Winds of Hastinapur* (HarperCollins *Publishers* India, 2013).

Madani, Rachida & (trans.) Hacker, Marilyn. *Tales of a Severed Head* (Yale University Press, 2012).

Menon, Ramesh. *The Mahabharata: A Modern Rendering, Vol. 1 & 2* (Rupa & Co, 2004).

Muddupalani & (trans.) Mulchandani, Sandhya. *The Appeasement of Radhika: Radhika Santawanam* (Penguin Books India, 2011).

Nagai, Mariko. *Georgic* (BkMk Press, 2010).

Nagarkar, Kiran. *Bedtime Story* (Fourth Estate – HarperCollins *Publishers*, 2015).

Nagra, Daljit. *Ramayana: A Retelling* (Faber & Faber Poetry, 2013).

Nair, M.T. Vasudevan & (trans.) Krishnankutty, Gita. *Bhima Lone Warrior* (Harper Perennial – HarperCollins *Publishers*, 2013).

Neelakantan, Anand. *Ajaya, Book I: Roll of Dice* (Platinum Press, 2013).

Pai, Anant (ed). *Stories from the Mahabharata: 5-in-1* (Amar Chitra Katha, 2009).

Pai, Anant (ed). *The Sons of the Pandavas: 3-in-1* (Amar Chitra Katha, 2005).

Panicker, Prem. *Bhimsen*, adaptation of M.T. Vasudevan Nair's *Randamoozham* (https://prempanicker.wordpress.com/2009/10/05/bhim-complete-and-unabridged/).

Patil, Amruta. *Adi Parva – Churning of the Ocean* (HarperCollins *Publishers* India, 2012).

Pattanaik, Devdutt. *Jaya: An Illustrated Retelling of the Mahabharata* (Penguin Books India, 2010).

Pattanaik, Devdutt. *The Pregnant King* (Penguin Books India, 2008).

Puri, Reena Ittyerah (ed). *The Mahabharata* (Amar Chitra Katha & Reader's Digest, 2010).

Rajagopalachari, C. *Mahabharata* (The Hindustan Times, 1969).

Ramanujan, A.K. *Three Hundred Ramayanas* (OPEN Magazine, October 2011).

Ramanujan, A.K., Rao, Velcheru Narayana & Shulman, David (ed. and trans.). *When God Is a Customer: Telugu Courtesan Songs by Ksetrayya and Others* (University of California Press, 1994).

Rao, Mani (trans.). *Bhagavad Gita: A Translation of the Poem* (Penguin Books India, 2011).

Ray, Pratibha & (trans.) Bhattacharya, Pradip. *Yajnaseni* (Rupa & Co, 1995).

Robertson, Robin. *The Hill of Doors* (Picador, 2013).

Rushdie, Salman. "The Disappeared", excerpted from *Joseph Anton* (*The New Yorker*, 17 September 2012).

Sawant, Shivaji and (trans.) Lal, P. & Nopany, Nandini. *Mrityunjay: The Death Conqueror* (Writers Workshop, 1989).

Singh, Jai Arjun. *Old Tales, New Renderings* (Himal Magazine, December 2006); *Epic*

Fictions: the Rashomon-like world of the Mahabharata (Jabberwock, August 2011); *Pop Goes the Epic* (Indian Quarterly, January-March 2014).

Subramaniam, Kamala. *Mahabharata* (Bhavan's Book University, 2012, 17th edition).

Tharoor, Shashi. *The Great Indian Novel* (Penguin Books India, 1990).

Tóibín, Colm. *The Testament of Mary: A Novel* (Scribner, 2012).

Tripathi, Salil. *The Colonel Who Would Not Repent: The Bangladesh War and Its Unquiet Legacy* (Aleph Book Company, 2014).

Varma, Pawan K. *Yudhishtar & Draupadi* (Penguin Books India, 1996).

Vatsyayana & (trans.) Daniélou, Alain. *The Complete Kama Sutra* (Park Street Press, 1994).

Vyaasa, Krishna Dwaipayana & (trans.) Ganguli, Kisari Mohan. *The Mahabharata, Vol 1-18* (http://www.sacred-texts.com/hin/maha/)

Winterson, Jeanette. *The Myth of Atlas and Heracles* (Canongate US, 2006).

FILMOGRAPHY

Bharat Ek Khoj (1988-89), television series. Based on *The Discovery of India* by Jawaharlal Nehru. Screenplay and dialogues: Vasant Dev, Ashok Mishra, Sandeep Pendse, Sunil Shanbag & Shama Zaidi. Cinematography: V.K. Murthy. Theme music: Vanraj Bhatia. Director & Producer: Shyam Benegal.

Coriolanus (2011). Playwright: William Shakespeare. Screenplay: John Logan. Cinematography: Barry Ackroyd. Music: Ilan Eshkeri. Director: Ralph Fiennes. Producers: Ralph Fiennes & John Logan.

Kalyug (1981). Screenplay: Shyam Benegal & Girish Karnad. Dialogues: Satyadev Dubey. Cinematography: Govind Nihalani. Music: Vanraj Bhatia. Director: Shyam Benegal. Producer: Shashi Kapoor.

Le mahâbhârata (1990), TV mini-series. Story: Vedavyas. Screenplay: Peter Brook, Jean-Claude Carrière, Marie-Hélène Estienne. Cinematography: William Lubtchansky. Music: Toshi Tsuchitori. Director: Peter Brook. Producer: Brooklyn Academy of Art & Channel Four Representative.

Mahabharat (1988-89), television series. Story: Vedavyas. Screenplay: Rahi Masoom Reza. Cinematography: Dharam Chopra. Director: B.R. Chopra & Ravi Chopra. Producer: B.R. Chopra.

Mahabharata (1965). Story: Vedavyas. Screenplay: Pandit Madhur & Vishwanath Pande. Dialogue: C.K. Mast. Cinematography: Narendra Mistry & Peter Pereira. Music: Chitra Gupta. Director: Babubhai Mistri. Producer: A.A. Nadiadwala.

Son Frère (2003). Story (novel): Philippe Besson. Adapted screenplay: Patrice Chéreau

& Anne-Louise Trividic. Cinematography: Eric Gautier. Editing: Françoise Gédigier. Director: Patrice Chéreau. Producer: Pierre Chevalier.

Thalapathi (1991). Screenplay, Story & Direction: Mani Ratnam. Cinematography: Santosh Sivan. Music: Illayaraja. Producer: G. Venkateswaran.

DANCE, THEATRE

Accumulation (1971). Choreography (and original performance): Trisha Brown. Sound: The Grateful Dead, *Uncle John's Band*. Production: Trisha Brown Dance Company. https://vimeo.com/12668671

Antigone (2012). Playwright: Jean Anouilh. Direction: Marc Paquien. Set design: Gérard Didier. Lighting: Dominique Bruguière. Sound Design: Xavier Jacquot. Costumes: Claire Risterucci. Production: Comédie-Française.

Beautiful Me (2005). Choreography: Gregory Maqoma in collaboration with Akram Khan, Faustin Linyekula, Vincent Mantsoe. Lighting: Michael Mannion. Radio script: Wole Soyinka. Costumes: Sun Goddess. Music: Poorvi Bhana, Bongani Kunene, Given Mphago, Isaac Molelekoa. Production: Gerald Bester for Centre national de la danse. http://www.numeridanse.tv/en/video/789_beautiful-me

Begin to Begin (2011). Choreography: Eva Recacha. Sound: Alberto Ruiz. Lighting design: Gareth Green. Costumes: Eleanor Sikorski. Commissioned by The Place Prize. https:// vimeo.com/21028593

Bit (2014). Concept & Choreography: Maguy Marin in collaboration with Ulises Alvarez, Kaïs Chouibi, Laura Frigato, Daphné Koutsafti, Mayalen Otondo/Cathy Polo, Ennio Sammarco. Lighting: Alexandre Béneteaud. Music: Charlie Aubry . Sets & Props: Louise Gros & Laura Pignon. Production: Compagnie Maguy Marin. http://www .numeridanse.tv/en/video/2427_bit

Des Témoins Ordinaires (2009). Concept: Rachid Ouramdane. Music: Jean-Baptiste Julien. Lighting: Yves Godin. Video: Jenny Teng & Nathalie Gasdoué. Costume & makeup: La Bourette. Producer: L'A. https://vimeo.com/28812422

Electra (2014). Playwright: Sophocles & (adaptation) Frank McGuiness. Direction: Ian Rickson. Design: Mark Thompson. Lighting: Neil Austin. Music: PJ Harvey. Sound: Simon Baker. Choreograpy: Maxine Doyle. Casting: Sam Jones CDG. Producer: Old Vic & Sonia Friedman Productions.

Empty Moves 1, 2, 3 (2014). Choreography: Angelin Preljocaj. Sound: John Cage, *Empty Words*. Producer: Ballet Preljocaj/ Le Pavillon Noir.

Fase, Four Movements to the Music of Steve Reich (1982). Choreography: Anne Teresa de Keersmaeker. Made with: Jennifer Everhard (Come Out) and Michèle Ann de Mey (*Piano Phase, Clapping Music*). Music: Steve Reich (*Piano Phase, Come Out, Violin Phase, Clapping Music*). Lighting: Mark Schwentner (*Violin Phase & Come Out*), Remon Fromont (*Piano Phase & Clapping Music*). Costumes: Martine André & Anne Teresa De Keersmaeker. Production: Schaamte, Avila (1982); Rosas & De Munt (1993). http://www.numeridanse.tv/en/video/1185_fase

Gnosis (2010). Artistic Director & Performer: Akram Khan. Guest artist: Fang-Yi Sheu. Musicians: Koushik Aithal, B C Manjunath, Kartik Raghunathan, Lucy Railton, Sanju Sahai, Bernard Schimpelsberger. Lighting: Fabiana Piccioli. Sound: Marcus Hyde. Costumes: Kei Ito, Kimie Nakano. Dramaturge: Ruth Little. Producer: Farooq Chaudhry for Khan Chaudhry Productions.

I Am the Wind (2011). Playwright: Jon Fosse. English translation: Simon Stephens. Direction: Patrice Chéreau. Choreographer/Artistic collaborator: Thierry Thieû Nang. Set design: Richard Peduzzi. Costumes: Caroline de Vivaise. Lighting: Dominique Bruguière. Sound design: Eric Neveux. Production: Young Vic (London) & Théâtre de la Ville (Paris). *http://www.theatre-video.net/video/I-Am-the-Wind-extruits*

In Your Rooms (2007). Choreography: Hofesh Shechter. Music: Hofesh Shechter & (music direction) Nell Catchpole, also featuring a sample from Takk... (Sigur Ros). Lighting design: Lee Curran. Costume design: Elizabeth Barker. Producer: Hofesh Shechter Company. https://www.youtube.com/ watch?v=QRtzM6mBL5k

La Nuit Juste Avant Les Forêts (2000). Playwright: Bernard-Marie Koltès. Director: Kristian Frédric. Set design: Enki Bilal. Featuring Denis Lavant.

Le Sacre du Printemps / Rite of Spring (1975). Choreography: Pina Bausch. Music: Igor Stravinsky. Collaboration: Hans Pop. Set & Costume: Rolf Borzik. Producter: Tanztheater Wuppertal / Pina Bausch. https://www.youtube.com/ watch?v=J4qm1wyzHwI

Le Sacre du Printemps / Rite of Spring (2014). Concept & choreography: Romeo Castellucci. Sound design: Scott Gibbons. Music: Igor Stravinsky. Recording, MusicAeterna, with musical direction by Teodor Currentzis. Artistic collaboration: Silvia Costa. Computer programming: Hubert Machnik. Producer: Ruhr Triennale. https://www .youtube.com/watch?v=PUKdhWdJaoc

Les Noces (1966). Choreography: Bronislava Nijinska. Music: Igor Stravinsky. Design: Natalia Gontcharova Producer: Royal Ballet (commissioned by Frederick Ashton). https://www.youtube. com/watch?v=vsXR81dLjjE&list=PL1AB6aSObxpd3 wCMBDz rpU281EmwPmbKo&index=12

Loin (2008). Concept & performance: Rachid Ouramdane. Music: Alexandre Meyer.

Video: Aldo Lee. Lighting: Pierre Leblanc. Costumes & makeup: La Bourette. Sets: Sylvain Giraudeau. Producer: L'A. https://www.youtube.com/ watch?v =3hUYD13CNFs

Kontakthof (1978). Choreography / Artistic direction: Pina Bausch. Set & Costume: Rolf Borzik. In collaboration with: Rolf Borzik, Marion Cito, Hans Pop. Music: Juan Llossas, Anton Karas, Sibelius and others... Producer: Tanztheater Wuppertal / Pina Bausch. https://www.youtube.com/watch?v=4ZbfsLW707I

MayBe (1981). Choreography: Maguy Marin. Music: Franz Schubert, Gilles de Binche, Gavin Bryars. Costume design: Louise Marin. Production: Compagnie Maguy Marin. https://www.youtube.com/watch?v=_pVc2100-eY

Noces (1989). Choreography: Angelin Preljocaj. Music: Igor Stravinsky. Score performed by Percussions de Strasbourg & Choeur contemporain d'Aix-en-Provence, conducted by Roland Hayrabedian. Costumes: Caroline Anteski. Lighting: Jacques Chatelet. Choreologists: Noémie Perlov, Dany Lévêque. Producer: Ballet Preljocaj. https://vimeo.com/68062364

Plexus (2012). Concept, direction & set design: Aurélien Bory. Choreography: Aurélien Bory & Kaori Ito. Performance: Kaori Ito. Music: Joan Cambon. Lighting: Arno Veyrat. Sound: Stéphane Ley. Costumes: Sylvie Marcucci. Dramatic art advisor: Taïcyr Fadel. Set technical conception: Pierre Dequivre. Producer: Compagnie 111 – Aurélien Bory. https://www. youtube.com/watch?v=9y_1uwZ7Mz4

Puz/zle (2012). Choreography: Sidi Larbi Cherkaoui. Music composition: Jean-Claude Acquaviva, Kazunari Abe, Olga Wojciechowska. Additional music: Bruno Coulais, Tavagna, traditional music from Corsica, Japan and the Middle East. Set design: Filip Peeters, Sidi Larbi Cherkaoui. Lighting: Adam Carrée. Video: Paul Van Caudenberg. Costume design: Miharu Toriyama. Producer: Eastman. http:// www.sadlerswells.com/ screen/video/2133409552001#

Soli (2006). Choreography: Anthony Egéa. Music: Tedd Zahmal. Lighting: Florent Blanchon. Performance: Emilie Sudre. Producer: Compagnie Rêvolution. https:// www.youtube.com/ watch?v=It8Nnvh2wjE

TeZukA (2011). Choreography: Sidi Larbi Cherkaoui. Music: Nitin Sawhney. Additional / traditional music: Tsubasa Hori, Woojae Park, Olga Wojciechowska. Set design & lighting: Willy Cessa. Calligraphy: Tosui Suzuki. Costume design: Sasa Kovacevic. Video: Taiki Ueda. Producer: Sadler's Wells, Bunkamura, Eastman. https://www .youtube.com/watch?v=plbEvqGNFOo

The Crimson House (2014). Choreography, concept, stage design & direction: Lemi Ponifasio. Lighting: Helen Todd. Production: MAU.

The Testament of Mary (2013). Playwright: Colm Tóibin. Director: Deborah Warner.

Performance: Fiona Shaw. Set design: Tom Pye. Costumes: Ann Roth. Lighting: Jennifer Tipton. Music & sound design: Mel Mercier. Producer: Barbican.

Umwelt (2004). Concept & Choreography: Maguy Marin in collaboration with Ulises Alvarez, Mary Chebbah, Teresa Cunha, Renaud Golo, Thierry Partaud, Cathy Polo, Denis Mariotte, François Renard, Jeanne Vallauri. Music/Sound design: Denis Mariotte. Lighting: Alexandre Béneteaud. Costumes: Cathy Ray. Production: Compagnie Maguy Marin. https://www.youtube.com/watch?v=S-cGS5oTWUo

Véronique Doisneau (2004). Concept: Jérôme Bel. With Véronique Doisneau. Excerpts of ballets by Jean Coralli & Jules Perrot (*Giselle*), Merce Cunningham (*Points in Space*), Mats Ek (*Giselle*), Rudolf Noureev (*La Bayadère* – Marius Petipa & *Le Lac des Cygnes* – Marius Petipa & Lev Ivanov). Commissioned and produced by l'Opéra national d Paris. https://www.youtube. com/watch?v=YoX6hn3RL9o

ACKNOWLEDGEMENTS

I thank the editors of the following publications in which certain poems from *Until the Lions* first appeared, sometimes in slightly different forms:

- *Poetry International Web* (December 2013): 'Constancy I, III, V & VI';
- *Indian Quarterly* (July 2015): 'Satyavati: Fault Lines II-IV';
- *The Wolf Magazine* (Summer 2014): 'Amba-Shikhandi: Manual for Revenge & Remembrance';
- *Granta 130: India* (January 2015): 'Shunaka: Blood Count';
- *Antiserious* (February 2015): 'Satyavati: Fault Lines VIII';
- *Blackbox Manifold no. 13* (Winter 2014): 'I. Blood Moon Rising: Poorna with Vyaasa' and 'II. Poorna to Satyavati: The Handmaid's Grail';
- *Scroll India* (March 2015): 'Ulupi: The Capillaries of Cosmic Bodies';
- *Almost Island* (Summer 2015): 'Krishna: Blueprint for a Victory'; 'Kunti: Ossature of Maternal Conquest & Reign'; 'Testament: Vrishali with Duryodhana';
- *The Caravan* (May 2012): 'Uttaraa: I. Life Sentences';
- *POEM* (Summer 2014): 'Uttaraa: II. To Abhimanyu: Memorabilia';
- *Prairie Schooner* (Volume 88, No. 4, Winter 2014): 'Uttaraa: III. Note to the Unborn Child'.

For the sanctuary, support – financial or infrastructural, always vital – and time they provided during the writing of this book, I am very thankful to

- Sangam House (India). specifically, for a residency in November 2012; for the close-knit community of writers it fosters;
- Wonju City and Toji Cultural Foundation (South Korea): for a residency across September-October 2013; for the generosity and reliable presence of the personnel Foundation;
- The Villa Départementale Marguerite Yourcenar and the Département du Nord (France): for a grant and a residency at the Villa in March 2015; for grand and caring hospitality; unforgettable vistas and possibly the finest, healthiest cuisine in France.

Abiding gratitude, more than I can express, to the many, many people who – in a myriad of ways – helped make this book a reality, among whom

- Karthika V.K.: for the five years of unflagging patience it took for an inchoate idea to become something slightly more; for not abandoning that idea despite my detours around dance scripts and productions, children's fables and hospitals; for numerous chocolate sorties that worked wonders with temporal glitches and diegetic voices; and a much-admired, gimlet gaze on all possible semantic, zoological and other anomalies, especially the poor beaver;
- James Byrne: for greeting 'Amba' so warmly – together with Sandeep Parmar – and giving her a cherished platform; for leading *Until the Lions* to another arc-en- ciel; for steadfast belief and encouragement and an eagle's eye, especially on the calendar;
- Shantanu Ray Chaudhuri, Ajitha G.S., Amrita Talwar, Prerna Gill, Bonita Shimray and Jojy Philip (in random order): for attention and expertise and unfailing good humour;
- Tony Ward, Angela Jarman and the team at Arc Publications: for the second chapter in this journey; for a beautifully produced book;
- Marielle Morin and Rick Simonson for their belief in these voices, for generously casting a bridge across the Atlantic Ocean;
- Anjali Singh of Ayesha Pande Literary for being at the other end of that bridge; for her immediate response, immense kindness, sparkling discussions and priceless counsel;
- Jill Schoolman at Archipelago Books: for her warmth and attentiveness in welcoming the lionesses to a new land and Emma Raddatz, for all the care, and unfailingly swift and thoughtful responses;
- The French Book Office, New Delhi & Prakriti Foundation: For continued support and warmth; for the invitation to India;
- Antony Gormley: for the generous loan of *Another Singularity* as cover for the Arc edition – a dream come true;
- Bryony McLennan and Philip Boot at Antony Gormley Studio: for their prompt and cheerful help with the formalities and technical elements;
- Pramod Kumar K.G.: for catalysing the cover image of the HC edition; for sourcing so much of the reference material and spotting ones I didn't know existed; for his dining table where ideas and poems germinate and where much soy milk and baingan bartha are consumed, though not together; mostly, for being – and the difference that makes to me;

- Mita Kapur and Siyahi: for the formalities;
- Marilyn Hacker, Sandeep Parmar, Anand Murty and Swarup B.R.: for repeated, close readings and insightful suggestions on time lines and voices, skeletal systems and connective tissue; for regular, valuable encouragement;
- David Shulman, Marilyn Hacker, Jeet Thayil, Alistair Spalding, Amit Chaudhuri and Thomas Meyer: for their time and words, both dearly cherished;
- R. Sivapriya, Priya Sarukkai Chabria, Juhi Saklani, Laetitia Zecchini and Kenneth Maennchen: for the early, lively discussions on multiple narratives;
- Sankar Mohan Radhakrishnan: for reading 'Satyavati: Fault Lines' with the grave focus and the red pen of the editorial martinet he is, despite the distractions provided by the content;
- Narayani Harigovindan, Vahni Capildeo, Siddhartha Bose, Arunava Sinha, Vivek Narayanan, Sumana Roy, Urvashi Butalia, Tishani Doshi, Arundhathi Subramaniam and Chandrahas Choudhury: for opportunities I wouldn't otherwise have dared to seek;
- Sreekishen Nair: for sharing scholarship on fascinating performing art and ritual practices and parallel belief systems sprung from the Mahabharata – all too often submerged in a majoritarian discourse;
- Retna Nair and Sukumaran Nair: for the patience and goodness to read out entire books aloud over Skype in the name of research;
- Ranvir Shah and Meera Krishnan: for procuring and dispatching a much-coveted copy of *Parva*; for the loan of *The Cult of Draupadi*;
- Leesa Gazi: for the conviction, very early on, that these voices clamoured to be staged;
- Françoise Gillard; for her fiery, fragile and luminous *Antigone* – inspiration to some of the voices in this collection;
- Farooq Chaudhry: for his immediate and unequivocal response to the early poems, his belief that they would be the right work for Akram Khan to explore and Akram Khan Company to produce;
- Jai Arjun Singh: for his own enduring Mahabharata obsession; for the months and years of feisty, intricate debate and dissections of character, motive, philosophy, politics and morality; for the kilogrammes of correspondence (that could well presage another book) on the many adaptations and retellings through time, from *Urubanga* to *Draupadi in High Heels*; for transforming this from a solitary, somewhat pathological endeavour to a decidedly more high-spirited, sometimes rollicking, peregrination;

- Koen Vandyke: for making it possible to carpe diem, though diem then was a bloodthirsty beast with too many fangs;
- The teams at St-Louis, Rothschild, André Mignot and Lariboisière Hospitals: for keeping me alive and relatively functional these last years; for being so fully invested in the everyday battle with EB and its attendant triffids;
- Sabine Kasbarian, Ginette Dansereau, Philippe Bruguière, Isabelle Pichon-Varin, Nicolas Renault, Marion Bastien, Nicolas Six, Adele and Bruce King, Sunithi Bhandari and Lakshman Rao: for reminding me of meals, and for ensuring these happened, even during the worst of triffid-attacks;
- Nandini Krishnan, Dawn Prentice, Adam Carrée and MJ: for laughter and cheer and memorable, if indefinable, meals in far-flung meridians;
- Pierre Marcolini and Pierre Hermé: without whose delicacies there wouldn't have been self-defined incentives and rewards for the completion of each voice, nor replenishment for fast-depleting grey cells;
- David Jays: for writing that lights up the dreariest of days;
- Mariko Nagai, Sally Altshuler, Rahul Soni, Karen Jennings and Raghu Karnad, my wonderful fellow Sangam-ites: for imagination and cheer and doubts and chatter and demons and dreams that provided the perfect Petri dish for wild ideas and surreal ghazals to breed;
- Sanjoy Roy: for attentiveness to – and shared delight in – form and structure, in poetry and in dance (especially *Vortex Temporum*); for being my 3 AM person on design and layout and blood-brain barriers breaches; for the discovery of ostinato and Shaken Udders, both of which had a marked impact on writing; and for a cornucopia of culinary treats in Islington, Holborn and St. Pancras;
- Anita Roy, the most resourceful, cheerful, incisive and rigorous of editorial Bonbibis: for presence and razor-sharp attention, precision and unfailing belief, for walking with this book from the first day to the last.